SLAVE ELF

CONNIE COCKRELL

Cover art by Autumn Raven, https://www.aravendesign.com

ISBN-13: 978-1797638102

Created with Vellum

*To my friends and readers who took the time to read Slave Elf
and give me the encouragement to keep going.*

ACKNOWLEDGMENTS

Slave Elf came about as a writing prompt from Chuck Wendig on his site, Terrible Minds. I was just going to write a quick, thousand word story. The story chose otherwise. I posted a thousand words for the story every week. Week after week, until a year later, I finally finished the book.

If you were one of my readers, (I mean you, Susie!) thank you. You stuck with me as I wandered, clueless, in the desert of story imagination, trying to figure out what this book wanted me to say.

I hope you all enjoy this much nicer version.

ALSO BY CONNIE COCKRELL

Lost Rainbows

Gulliver Station Box Set

A New Start

The Challenge

Hard Choices

Revolution

Brown Rain Series: First Encounter

The Downtrodden

Kindred Spirits

Tested

The Jean Hays Series: Mystery at the Fair

Mystery in the Woods

Mystery at the Book Festival

Mystery at the Reunion (coming soon!)

The Bad Seed

Recall

Halloween Tales: A Collection of Stories

Christmas Tales: A Collection of Stories

CHAPTER 1

"This must all seem confusing to you, Delia." Lord Traford looked at Master Corpet and then to his own son, Sir Alexis. They both nodded to the Lord. "We have a matter of some consequence to discuss with you."

Delia placed her glass of sherry on the low table centered in front of them and folded her hands in her lap to keep them from shaking. They were also locked together to keep her from reaching up and trying to pull up the embarrassingly low neckline of the dress Master Corpet had her wear to this dinner. She'd never worn anything so fine as this dark blue silk dress. She'd had all she could do all evening, though, to keep from dropping her dinner on it or tripping over the hem. She was already perched on the edge of her chair from nervousness, after they'd called her away from the rest of the ladies to the Lord's library. Lord Traford's comment scared her. She was only Master Corpet's bookkeeping slave and secretary. Being commanded to put on such a fancy dress and attend dinner with nobles had been frightening enough.

"Master Corpet reminds me that you've been with the caravan over sixty years now. A whole lifetime for men."

Delia's mouth went dry. Fear washed through her. And dread. What was coming? She looked at Master Corpet, seated in a deep, dark brown leather armchair as though it was an everyday event. Lord Traford's son, Sir Alexis, who'd poured sherry for her from a small bar table in the corner, stood, one arm on the mantel of an elaborately carved fireplace, empty this time of year except for a screen with a hunting dog scene on it, his drink near his elbow. Both of them seemed eager. She turned her attention back to the Lord, himself, who sat in what was obviously his favorite chair, a match to hers.

"We believe it's time to let you in on our secret."

Delia nodded. She couldn't trust her voice not to quaver. *I looked around the library again. So many books.* She was envious he had shelves and shelves of books. They made her tiny collection, sitting on a high shelf in her wagon, look pathetic.

Lord Traford sipped his whiskey and replaced it on the table. "My grandfather is the one who put you into Master Corpet's care."

Her heart beat began to race. *Care? How was making me a slave, care?*

What she was thinking must have shown on her face. *I was going to have to watch that.* She schooled her face into neutral. Who knew what a great Lord would or could do to a lowly slave? Traford raised his hand. "Please, I know that sounds strange, but it's true. Your parents gave you to my grandfather for a reason."

Delia's hands twisted in her lap as a roaring filled her ears. *My parents gave me up? What?*

"I'm sorry. I'm making a bungle of this. What I mean is, they gave you to my grandfather to hide you. It seemed to him, and to *his* father," he nodded again to Corpet, "that no one would look for you in a slaver's caravan."

She stared at Corpet. He nodded. "It's true, Delia. You were in great danger if you had stayed with your parents. I've done my best for you, I have, since I took over the caravan from my grandfather and father, I have."

She thought back to Emil, Corpet's horse master, who had made her life a misery since he joined the caravan. It was not uncommon for him to ride up beside her wagon and strike her on the thigh with his quirt, then dash off, laughing, as she nursed the pain. *That is the best Corpet can do?* She clenched her teeth together and shrugged, then turned back to Lord Traford, doing her best to hide her anger. After sixty years of training as a slave, she must not so easily forget her place, even though she was an elf.

"What danger, my Lord?"

"What do you know about the Elves?"

Delia struggled not to snort at the evasive question. "Not much. I haven't been allowed to talk to them. I've had no instruction and have read no histories about them." Her voice revealed how angry she was, and she shuddered to think how impertinent her behavior was. Would there be punishment for such daring?

The Lord nodded, but she could see an eyebrow twitch. She was going to have to keep her voice under control.

"Were you aware the Elves, like us humans, have a king?" She nodded.

"King Ucheni is his name. The Queen is Ralae. For the last sixty-five years, they have been fighting, defending the kingdom against his uncle, Iyuno, who started a civil war to claim the throne. It has been a struggle, but the king's advisors have been waiting for a prophecy to come to fruition."

Lord Traford sipped his whiskey and resettled himself in his chair.

Sir Alexis had moved to a small sofa, draped his right leg over his left and seemed bored. Master Corpet was studying her, sitting forward, eager, almost. *What is the rest of the story?*

The Lord continued. "The prophecy is that a black-haired savior will come to them. More powerful than any elf in two thousand years, the savior will settle all arguments and bring peace to the land."

"How do they know the prophecy is true?"

"They had a sign, sixty-five years ago."

All three men were watching her. Waiting for something. "What was the sign?"

"A black-haired child was born to the Queen."

Delia's mind spun as her hand touched a long tendril of her black hair. She blinked. She felt faint. "You mean…"

He nodded. "Yes, Delia. It's you." He inclined his head. "Your Highness."

She sat very still, numb. The struggle to grasp the fact that she had a family and that they were at war and that they were royalty was too much to bear. Finally, a clear thought came to her. "I don't have any powers."

"Your parents mentioned that you would begin to see them manifest at this age." Lord Traford tugged his lace-hemmed sleeves down inside his brocade jacket. "I have acquired a tutor to help you through this period of learning to use them."

She looked at Master Corpet. "You mean I'm no longer a slave?" Her heart began to race as her hands twisted in her lap.

"That is true, though to me, you were never a slave. A

ward, would be the best way to put it." He grinned at her as though he was pleased with himself.

A wave of anger washed over Delia that made her gasp. *A ward? Really?* She shot up from her seat and struggled to keep her anger in check. *Controlled like a dog for decades. Leered at by your men. Whipped by Emil. Locked in my wagon when elves were near.* "Never a slave?" It embarrassed her that her voice quavered. "A ward?" Her last comment came out with more venom than she wanted. She made an effort to keep her hands from turning into fists. Keeping her voice low and calm she said, "And now I find out I'm a princess and have a people and I'm supposed to be their savior?" Despite her struggles, her voice rose a few notes. "I don't know what or who they are?"

Lord Traford's face fell. "We were trying to keep word of you from the elf king's uncle."

She turned on Master Corpet. "Your horse master delights in spurring up to my wagon so he can whip me on the leg. Then he laughs as he dashes away." Her face burned with the memory of the pain she'd had to nurse and keep to herself.

"Whipped?" Corpet's face turned red with shock. "No one was to touch you. Ever."

Delia barely restrained another snort. "Emil thinks it's funny." She folded her arms over her chest, trying to contain her fury.

All three men stood up. Lord Traford placed a hand over his heart. "Ma'am. Please forgive us.

We made the best arrangements we could. We've sent periodic reports back to the king that you were well, and learning languages and mathematics and writing."

Corpet put out a hand. It was meant to be a comfort, but involuntarily, she stepped out of his reach. Then she paced the length of the room and back again, nearly tripping over the skirt of the elegant blue gown she was unused to wearing, finally stopping in front of the Lord. After a deep breath, she again made her voice calm.

"What's next then?" It still came out angry. Her eyes were on the floor as, while stressed, her mind made note of the pattern of flowers woven into the rug she stood on. How she had the nerve to talk to him in that tone of voice was a matter to think about later.

Lord Traford cleared his throat. "I have an apartment prepared for you, here in the palace. I've arranged for you to meet your tutor tomorrow after breakfast."

She closed her eyes. Her greatest dream, freedom, was coming true. She was not a slave, but she didn't feel like a princess. All she could think about were her pitiful possessions in the wagon. "What about my things?"

"They'll be sent, first thing in the morning," Corpet rushed to say. "I'm sorry for causing you so much pain, Delia. It was never my intention."

She opened her mouth to smooth it over, as she would have as a slave. She bit back the first comment that came to mind and said instead, "Intention or not, it happened." *My entire childhood was spent making myself small and invisible. No parents, no love.* She shook with the pent-up emotion.

He looked devastated. She didn't care.

Sir Alexis intervened. "Princess Delia."

She whirled to face him, sure that she would now be punished for all of her impertinence.

"I'm sure Master Corpet did the best he could, given the circumstances. We're all a little out of our depths here. It must be very disconcerting for you, especially."

That, at least, is true. Her entire reality had just been shifted. She reached down and picked up her sherry, draining the glass. From slave to princess in a single sentence. She drew a deep breath as she put the glass back on the table. In a conciliatory tone of voice she asked, "May I retire to my apartment?"

All three men began nodding and making apologetic noises. "I'll lead you," Sir Alexis said. He went to the door and held it open.

"My Lord. Master." She nodded to Corpet and Lord Traford and left the room, checking behind her to gage their reactions. She couldn't believe she'd gotten away with such disrespect or that they were doing their best to be conciliatory in their turn.

As Sir Alexis guided her through the palace, up another flight of marble stairs and along a long hall, she pondered the effect of the change from Delia as a slave to Delia as princess. *Strong words from a princess don't get punished.*

He stopped at the last door on the right and opened the double doors. "I do hope you find everything to your liking."

They entered a sitting room. A circle of armchairs surrounded a low table, similar to the arrangement in the library she had just left but in fabric, not leather, and in feminine pastels, primarily greens and blues. She turned slowly to see landscape paintings hung on the pale green walls and a bookcase filled with volumes centered on the wall to her right. Opposite the door was a bank of windows with a window seat cushioned and pillowed to match the armchairs. To the right of the windows was an open door where she found her bedroom and walked inside.

Here again, wide windows spanned a window seat, and a bed wide enough to sleep four people stood opposite the door. All Delia could think about was her cramped bed, inches too short, on one end of her wagon. She would be able to stretch out as much as she liked!

A dressing table was on the wall with the door. Opposite

the window, a fireplace faced two armchairs upholstered in the same fabric as in the sitting room. She could fit three caravan wagons in the bedroom alone. The opulence was beyond anything she had ever imagined. "This is nice."

Sir Alexis bowed. "Mother did her best to make the rooms pleasing to you."

Pleasing? They were so much more than pleasing that she had no idea what to say. She settled on, "I'll thank her when I see her." Suddenly she was exhausted. "Thank you for showing me the apartment."

"My pleasure." He backed out of the room. "I shall leave you now, to your rest."

Delia followed him to the door.

"There's a bell pull next to your bed and one here." He pointed to a long ribbon of fabric hanging by the door to the hall. "Just pull it if you need anything, and a servant will be here shortly."

"I appreciate that." Just pull the ribbon and someone would come running. Who would have thought that?

"Breakfast is at nine, but if you wish, you can have the servants bring you something earlier."

"Very thoughtful." She was overwhelmed. How she could think of anything to reply to the young man was a mystery to her.

He stepped into the hall. "Good night, Princess."

"Sleep well, Sir." He bowed again and closed the doors.

She stood, her back against the door, as she surveyed the room again. Candles were everywhere, and beeswax candles at that. Such extravagance she never in her life had seen. She couldn't fathom the cost just in this room.

Back in the bedroom she explored the wardrobe. Several dresses hung there, along with matching pairs of shoes. The dresser held undergarments, bedclothes and dressing gowns.

She pulled a nightgown from the drawer and changed. As she took down her hair and brushed it out with a silver-backed brush she found on the dressing table, she tried to sort out what had happened to her.

I have a family. Parents anyway. Did I have brothers or sisters? Then there was an uncle, great-uncle, she supposed, who was challenging her father, the king, for the throne. On top of all of that, she was supposed to have powers. What could those be? She had been purposely hidden. With a slave caravan. Purposely kept ignorant of her people. Why?

There were so very many questions and no answers.

CHAPTER 2

After a restless night, Delia rose just as the sun began to brighten the eastern sky. Pink and blue clouds were changing gradually to yellow, then orange, as the sun came up over the city towers. She washed in the cold water left for her and put on a blue dress from the wardrobe and found shoes to match. They fit perfectly. As she ran my hands down the fine material, which had a subtle dark green design woven into the fabric, she idly wondered how Lady Traford knew her size.

Standing in front of the full-length mirror—another opulence she had trouble accepting—she realized she no longer looked like the slave girl, dressed in roughly woven dirt-colored skirt and blouse. The image reflected back at her was a princess, but she still didn't feel like one. Dressed, she rang the pull next to her bed and went into the sitting room.

She opened the curtains there and watched the sun rise until a soft knock sounded at the door. "Come in."

The door opened to reveal a young woman. She was discreetly dressed in a dove gray gown, a white apron over all, her black hair pulled back and put up in a bun at the back of her head. She stepped into the room, closing the door behind her. "You rang, Princess?"

She had to recover at the honorific. It was still too strange. "Yes." Delia swallowed, unaccustomed to giving orders. "What's your name?"

"Priscilla, Ma'am." She bowed her head.

"Priscilla, Lord Traford mentioned to me that I could get an early breakfast served here." The girl didn't seem surprised, so she continued. "Something light. I'll attend breakfast with the Lady Traford, later."

"Yes, Princess." She turned to leave.

"Wait."

Priscilla turned back toward her, hands folded in front of her apron. "Ma'am."

Delia felt so awkward. "Have you been up all night waiting for a call from me?"

"No, Ma'am. I came on duty an hour ago. Lady Traford thought you might rise early, this being a new place to you. I'll be your personal maid for the time being."

She stared at her. *A maid? For me? She hardly looks old enough.* "How old are you, Priscilla?"

"Twenty, Ma'am."

She seemed so solemn. "Thank you, Priscilla."

The girl turned and left.

Delia sat in the window seat and watched the city wake. The sunlight hit a crystal globe on the polished wooden table in front of the window seat. Rainbows danced on the walls around the sitting room. She realized there something etched within the ball and she picked it up and peered inside. Elven letters, she could see, though the script was so elaborate she couldn't read it. Her stomach churned. She felt like an imposter. These people were soon going to realize that's what she was, even the servant, Priscilla. *She belonged here, not me.* She cradled the cold crystal to her bosom, trembling as a panic made her hands shake and her stomach roll. *All this space!* It was too much.

She backed into the corner of the window seat, knees to chest and the crystal held close, as the room spun and grew and shrank in turns until her breathing was coming in great gulps. She closed her eyes and focused on the warmth of the sun on her face. That was familiar. Comforting. Then the globe also became warm. Welcoming.

As her breathing slowed, she opened her eyes. The room was now just a room. Big, yes. But not so frightening. She stroked the globe and thought it twinkled at her. She stared long and hard into its center, but it didn't do anything again. She put it back in its little holder and returned to the seat to continue watching the city.

When Priscilla returned, she had a tray with her. "On the window seat, Princess, or on the table?"

"The window seat, please."

She carried the tray over and placed it at the opposite end of the cushion. "Shall I pour, Princess?"

"No, I can do it. Please, pull a chair over and sit with me." She saw an eyebrow twitch, but the girl nodded and carried over a small chair and placed it near the tray, facing her. That let Delia know she was doing something wrong. No help for it now but to press on. Maybe she could find out some information.

"Good. Thank you. Tell me how long you've been in service here." She poured tea for herself, then selected some cut fruit, a square of orange cheese and a roll, and pulled them all over in front of herself.

"Three years, Ma'am. My father indentured me to Lord Traford."

"I see." Delia blew across the tea cup and sipped. It was a

nice dark tea, with a floral and citrus undercurrent. Perfect for breakfast. "And what do you do here?"

"I worked in the kitchen, at first, scut work. Then the housekeeper moved me to cleaning rooms. She must have liked my work because later I became Lady Traford's third maid. Occasionally I served visiting ladies. Now I am your maid." She studied her hands, folded in her lap when she had finished.

"You must be very clever, or they wouldn't have promoted you so quickly."

Priscilla shrugged. "So it seems. I do my work well and keep what I hear to myself."

She nodded. "Discretion is a valuable characteristic." Delia knew from keeping Master Corbet's counsel how much it was valued. "Would you rather not be my maid?"

"I do as I'm told, Princess." Her eyes stayed on her hands.

"And what have you been told to do?" Delia wondered if she was a spy for Lord Traford. If she was, would she tell her?

Priscilla raised her head. "Follow your orders for your care and well-being. Keep your apartment clean and tidy. Care for your clothing and person. Run errands for you if needed."

Delia broke off a bit of cheese and bread and chewed them while she thought. "And what are you supposed to report to Lord Traford?"

"I've been given no instruction on that, Princess."

Whether she had or not, sooner or later his Lordship would want to know what she was thinking and saying. She nodded to her. "I don't have any instruction for you except to come back at nine and escort me to breakfast. I don't know my way around the house yet. After breakfast, I'm to meet a tutor. I have no idea how long that will take, or if lessons will begin immediately. In any case, if you can determine my schedule, I'd appreciate you being there at the end of the meeting or the lesson, to bring me back here. Eventually I'll know my way around and won't need that type of hand-holding."

"Yes, Princess."

Priscilla calling her "Princess" was strange. She rolled the title around in her head, trying to come to grips with it. It was still too odd. "I don't require a lot of care, Priscilla. Mostly escort until I learn my way around, and caring for my apartment and clothing. I suspect I won't have time to do those things myself."

Her eyebrows rose at the last statement.

She chuckled. "I've been caring for myself for a long time, Priscilla. Trust me that I do know how."

The girl nodded. "Yes, Princess."

She wiped her hands on the linen napkin and placed it on the tray. "Have you eaten?"

"No, Princess."

Waving at the tray, Delia said, "Help yourself. You brought more than enough."

Her eyes went wide. "Oh no, Princess. That's unacceptable. I shouldn't even be sitting in your presence."

She closed her eyes and took a deep breath. Of course not. Standards must be maintained. She looked her in the eyes. "I apologize, Priscilla. I won't presume again."

She could hear a tiny sigh of relief as Priscilla inclined her head. "Thank you, Princess."

"I'm finished. You can take the tray away and go get your breakfast."

She rose from the chair and put it back where it belonged. Picking up the tray she said, "I'll return at nine."

"That will be fine. Thank you, Priscilla."

She bowed and left the apartment. Delia leaned against the wall, staring out over the city. Sunlight touched the high points, inching its way down the walls to the streets below where early morning vendors were beginning to open shops and pull carts into the streets.

A day ago that girl wouldn't have even looked at me. Housemaids to lords and ladies were as far up the social scale from a slave as was Lord Traford to Corpet. Now she was telling the girl what to do. True, Corpet had ordered her to deliver his orders to Sam, his servant boy, and even to Emil. But it wasn't her issuing the orders. Still, they called her "princess" and were considering her feelings. A strange situation at best. She could feel her stomach knot with stress over what the morning would bring.

CHAPTER 3

At a few minutes after nine, Delia was led into the breakfast room. Sir Alexis Traford was at the buffet along the right-side wall, selecting morsels from chafing dishes to put on his plate. Lady Traford came in behind her.

"Good morning, Princess Delia." The lady stopped and gave her a peck on the cheek then took her arm.

Delia had all she could do not to recoil. No one had ever greeted her like that before.

"How did you sleep?"

"Well enough, Lady Traford. Thank you for asking." She nodded at Sir Alexis as he turned from the buffet. "Good morning, Sir Alexis."

"Good morning, Your Highness." He smiled as he sat down. "I'm glad you're joining us."

The Lady walked Delia to the buffet. "We keep breakfast casual. Serve yourself whatever you'd like." She nodded in the direction of a uniformed man at the door at the back of the room. "Lors will pour tea, coffee, juice, or water, as you indicate."

Delia wondered at the quantity of servants. What on earth did they each do all day?

The breakfast went on longer than she cared. She managed to make at least three errors in etiquette that she could see, judging from Lors's reactions. Maybe more. Finally, Sir Alexis finished and offered to take Delia to the tutor.

He led her out of the small dining room. Priscilla was waiting outside of the door.

"Sir Alexis is taking me to the tutor, Priscilla. Thank you for waiting."

"Yes, ma'am."

"She'll be in the conservatory, Priscilla." Sir Alexis held out his arm. "Shall we proceed?"

"Certainly." Delia did her best to quiet the butterflies in her stomach. She was glad she hadn't eaten much.

On the way, Sir Alexis entertained her with stories about the portraits and landscapes of ancestors and famous battles on the walls. She arrived at the conservatory relaxed.

The space was huge, walled on three sides with glass. It was lush and green and humid, a definite change from the desert environment where Katzin, Lord Traford's city, was located. Delia tried to take in all of the different flowering plants as Sir Alexis walked her around the central pool and plantings to an open set of glass double doors on the fourth wall. Just inside stood a small wrought-iron table and chairs, a tea tray in the middle, with a view to a lawn and garden outside. It was very lovely.

A man sat at the table, looking out. He turned at the approach of Sir Alexis and Delia, and rose as they neared.

Delia's breath caught in her throat. It was an elf, and she had been keeping him waiting. Her heart began to beat so hard she thought Sir Alexis could hear it.

The elf had long blond hair—silver at the temples—pulled back on the sides to a braid that fell over the back hair that hung below his broad shoulders. His deep brown eyes, with flecks of gold in the irises, and high cheek-bones, made his face seem aristocratic. A tooled leather belt at his waist bearing a silver dragon buckle set off the sage-green tunic. His fawn colored breeches were tucked into knee-high brown leather boots. He wore a silver pin, a sigil of a spreading tree, on his left breast.

It was Delia's first close look at an elf. Her heart seemed caught in her throat, for he was everything she had ever dreamed an elf would look like.

"Lord Enaur, this is Delia, Princess of the house of Ucheni. Your Highness, this is Lord Enaur, an elf of renown, from your father's kingdom." Sir Alexis bowed as he stepped back.

She could hardly take her eyes off of the elf. He studied her. "Welcome back, Princess."

"Thank you, My Lord Enaur." Her mouth was nearly too dry to speak. Was she supposed to curtsy? No, that wouldn't work. She was supposed to be a princess.

"Will you have tea with me?" he asked as he indicated the tray beside them.

Her knees felt like water. "Yes. Certainly." She gripped the back of the chair next to her and controlled herself as she sat.

"I'll take my leave, then." Sir Alexis bowed to Delia, then the elf, turned and left through the open doors.

She clasped her hands in her lap to control the trembling. Her first meeting with an elf and she had no idea what to say.

Enaur sat and poured tea for both of them. They were silent through the adding of cream and sugar. Once his cup was to his satisfaction and he'd replaced it in the saucer, he took a breath.

"I've been informed that you were told who you are just last night." He studied her face. "It must have been a shock."

At last, something she could talk about. She nodded. "It was. It is. I'm having difficulty rearranging what I thought about my life until now."

He sipped again. "Please. Drink your tea." He looked around the conservatory. "Then we'll walk around the gardens and I'll give you more background."

Delia picked up her cup and sipped. This was a more robust tea than the one she'd had for breakfast. Fortifying. She glanced around the conservatory. Did he suspect listeners? She emptied the cup so as not to keep him waiting.

He rose and held out his hand. She took it and rose beside him. "I have much to share, and a message from your parents."

They left the brick-floored conservatory and stepped out onto the green lawn. What could the message be?

CHAPTER 4

H e dropped Delia's hand as they strolled past flower beds and stately trees. "Your parents send both greet- ings and apologies. I take it you do not know much about what is going on in the Elven Kingdom?"

That was nice of them, she thought with more than a little scorn. Delia shook her head. *Perhaps they're in earnest. I should give them a chance.* "I know a little, from market gossip, but Master Corpet kept news of elves to himself." She took a breath, "Or at least away from me. I was told there's a civil war."

Enaur nodded. "Your great-uncle and your father have never gotten along well. He resented being second-born of your great-grandfather, always considering himself smarter and stronger in magic than your grandfather or father." He clasped his hands behind his back as they stopped to admire a bed of blue iris. "It's unfortunate. King Ucheni is a just and noble king. Fair and kind-hearted. He doesn't have your Uncle Iyuno's magical powers, that's true, but it doesn't make him less of a good king."

"And this prophecy?"

"Yes. It came to my mother, back in your great-great-grandfather's reign. Your house and mine have a centuries-old bond." He shook his head. "A child at the time, she went into a trance in the middle of court, shouted out the prophecy and collapsed. It was three days until she regained herself and remembered what had happened. The court was in an uproar."

The pair moved on from the iris bed. "Your grandfather being dead, Iyuno believed he was to be the next King, but your great-grandfather promoted Ucheni instead, insisting that whatever trouble was coming would be best handled by a younger elf. That's when Iyuno began plotting. It was your birth that set him off. By the time you were a toddler, Ucheni and Ralae agreed that you must be hidden from your great-uncle. They concocted the plan with the previous Lord Traford. Then, when I'd heard what Traford had done," he sighed, "well, there was nothing to be done. Making a fuss would have drawn attention to you."

Delia saw him wrinkle his nose. "You didn't approve?"

Enaur shrugged. "It was against my advice. But I serve your father faithfully, so I arranged everything." He shook his head. "I apologize. I do. It could not have been easy living amongst the humans."

"I didn't really know anything else. It just was," she shrugged, "I'd have snatches of memories of a happier time. Laughter and music."

He grimaced. "But you were safe?"

"Safe enough." A quick flash of Emil's laughter at the quick, smart sting of his quirt shot through her memory, but she pushed it down. She was done with that. She was a princess now, right?

"I did have watchers along Corpet's route, that reported back and confirmed what he and Traford were saying."

She nodded. It felt good. Reassuring, perhaps, that someone had been watching out for her after all.

They reached the back wall of the estate. Delia noticed the trees planted to hide the wall. It occurred to her the Trafords lived in as much of a prison as she had. "And powers? I've never noticed any powers in myself."

Enaur faced her. "It's subtle, at first. Things happen that you don't recognize or even realize. Most elves, growing up in homes where magic is performed all around them, manifest early, little powers, like the sight, foreseeing events that will happen to them, or an ability to guide plant growth or work with metal." He studied her. "You never noticed any of that?"

"No." Delia shook her head. "I have an ability with numbers, accounts, languages. There really wasn't any plant-growing or metal-work going on around me." She thought briefly of saying that she had spent most of her time doing her best to be invisible, but that sounded petty and whiny, so she kept her peace.

He nodded. "You may be manifesting in the languages or numbers, since that's what you've been exposed to. Let us try an experiment."

Delia's heart quickened. What would they find as they probed her power? She took a breath. "Very well."

"Relax and close your eyes. Focus inward, shutting out your thoughts, your fears, the touch of the wind and the sounds around us. Empty your mind and focus inward. Relax into a nothingness." His voice progressively softened until he could barely be heard.

Delia slowly relaxed her mind, then shut out the sounds around her. It was difficult; her mind wanted to analyze everything happening. She refocused at every stray thought, quieting that analysis, letting her arms and body relax, softening her face. It seemed she heard a humming. Not from without, but within. A soothing sound, pleasant but strong. She followed the sound into herself, allowing herself to be led, unquestioningly.

It was a light, she saw. A glow, really, at her core. Soft yet strong, her center. Delia reached out to it and as her mind touched it, it flashed. A wave of heat and light, joy and gratitude, overcame her. Delia staggered and her eyes opened as Enaur caught her by her arms.

"Are you all right, Princess?"

Delia gasped. "It was so beautiful!"

Enaur smiled. "Good. Good. I'm glad your first effort was successful. You've unlocked your power. And well done." He walked her to a nearby bench and they sat down. "Young elves tap into their power early, without that opening. Sometimes they get blocked and must try several times to reach their center."

Delia trembled on the bench. The world seemed both brighter and duller than it had a moment ago. She mentioned it to Enaur.

"Your magical sight has opened. You see the world both new-made, yet at the same time, not as lovely as the magic at your core. That will resolve itself. You will see more in the world now than you ever have." He looked around the garden. The world is a lovely place, the plants and animals, the beautiful and the ugly, it's all a balance, and magical in its own right. You have much to learn."

"I look forward to it."

On the walk back to the conservatory she realized many of the plants now had auras, or at least now she could see them. A rabbit hopped out from some bushes and froze when it saw them. She could see an aura around it as well. "I see auras sparkling around the plants and animals."

"That's good. It won't be long before you stop seeing it

uninvited. You'll be able to call on that power at will to see a creature's aura. Right now, just opened, it comes unbidden."

She smiled. "Will there be another lesson today?"

Enaur shook his head. "The opening is enough for today. Tomorrow we'll resume your lessons. I expect it won't take long for you to gain your full powers."

CHAPTER 5

Delia nodded. Now that he mentioned it, she was a little tired. "When will I go to see my parents?"

"After you have full power. The king and queen want you to be able to defend yourself before you go back. They look forward to seeing you."

Delia nodded. She wondered if they really did look forward to seeing her. There had been no contact at all since she'd been dropped at Corpet's.

"They missed you terribly."

The statement caught her by surprise. As though he could read her mind.

"Your aura gives you away."

She blushed. "I hope one of the lessons is on how to control that." What she didn't want was for every passing elf to know what she was feeling.

"Not really. It's just that we stop looking for each elf's or creature's aura." He shrugged. "I just meant that they are looking forward to meeting you and that they missed you. It was not an easy decision to hide you away. The threat from Iyuno was great enough against you to warrant it."

"I'll take you at your word." He, Lord Traford, and Master Corpet all kept saying that her great-uncle was a threat, but in her experience, her biggest threat had come from the caravanner men. She remembered a night, just a few days ago, huddling in her wagon while the laughter and drumming, the shouts of the caravanner men to the dancing slaves, rolled in through the small open windows of the wagon. It was too hot to shut them. She had pulled the collar of her nightgown closer to her neck and shuddered. She knew what was going to happen, probably was already happening to those dancing girls.

With a sigh, she had rolled out of bed and lit the tiny brazier, putting the teapot over the flame. If she couldn't sleep, she might as well finish the caravan master's letter to the next city's Lord. She lit the lamp and sat down, the unfinished letter on the small table in front of her. The current master was the third she'd been held by, all sons or grandsons of her original owner. She sharpened the quill. In elf-years she knew she was still quite young, stolen from some elf encampment as a very young child. Even so, she could read and write in elvish, dwarvish, and in multiple languages of men. That, at least, came easy to her.

The master had made sure she was left alone, for the most part, and she was grateful for that bit of courtesy. Caravanners are not the most genteel of men.

She gave herself a little shake out of her memories as they arrived back at the conservatory. Priscilla was sitting at the table with a piece of embroidery, a tray of glasses and a ewer of water ready for them. She rose and bowed. "Princess, Lord Enaur. Water?"

"No thank you." Enaur shook his head. "I'll take my leave, Princess. Same time tomorrow, here?"

"Yes, Sir. Tomorrow."

He bowed and left, going through the conservatory and to the house. Delia wondered if he was going to report to Lord Traford.

"Water, Princess?"

Delia took her mind from Enaur and sat down. "Yes please." She could see that Priscilla's aura was a rosy pink. Sparkles danced all around her. Even the water had sparkles. Priscilla put the glass in front of her. Delia's hand trembled a bit as she reached for it. She wondered at the water's sparkles, frothing up out of the glass and spilling down the sides, over her hand. Musing, she drank, wondering if she'd feel the sparkles. She didn't, and was a little disappointed. "I hope I haven't kept you waiting too long," she said as she put the glass back down.

"No, Princess. I had a bit of embroidery to keep me occupied."

"May I see it?"

Priscilla took the piece in its hoop from the table and handed it to Delia.

"It's a handkerchief." Delightedly, Delia examined the stitching. It was a leaf and flower pattern, in yellows and greens, the stitches small and even. Of course there had been no one in the caravan to teach her such crafts. "It's beautiful."

"My grandmother taught me." Priscilla took back the work and dropped it into an apron pocket.

"Would you teach me?"

The young woman's eyes widened. "Certainly, Princess. I'll gather the materials and find a suitable piece for you to begin learning on."

Delia realized her trembling had stopped. "I look forward to it." She looked around the conservatory. "Do you know all of the flower names in here?"

Priscilla shook her head. "No, Princess. Shall I arrange for the gardener to explain?"

"That would be wonderful. Yes, please. Later this afternoon, or tomorrow, perhaps, as his time is available."

"I will arrange it, Princess."

Delia rose. "Let's tour the house, Priscilla. It's foolish for me to have to be guided everywhere."

Priscilla smiled. "Yes, Princess."

They spent an hour and a half exploring all of the parts of the house—including the kitchens—that Priscilla had access to. They arrived back in Delia's rooms in the early afternoon.

"Dinner is at seven, Princess. Would you like a lunch to tide you over?"

"Yes please. And tea."

Priscilla nodded and left.

Delia sat in the window seat and looked out over the wall of the estate. She was a little surprised at how extensive the grounds were here in the middle of Katzin. From her window she could see the desert beyond the town, a striking contrast to the lush gardens on the grounds.

She was lost in thought over her morning's lesson when Priscilla returned with a tray. "I brought an assortment, Princess, until I learn your preferences." She put the tray on the low table, then shut the room door. Delia went to one of the chairs near the table and sat down. "What did you bring me?"

Priscilla raised the cover. "A salad of greens with sliced apple, raisins and nuts, a plate of cheese and cold cuts, rolls, chutney, butter, mustard, and a bowl of mixed cut fruit."

A knock sounded at the door. Priscilla answered it and brought in another tray. This one had hot tea service and carafes of water, iced tea, and a red and a white wine. "I know you asked for tea, Princess, but I thought you may like these to be here for the afternoon."

"How thoughtful, Priscilla."

She ate a little of everything. Delia seemed particularly hungry, though in the caravan, she never had a mid-day meal. Perhaps it was the awakened magic. "Thank you, Priscilla."

The young woman nodded and took the tray of leftover food back to the kitchens.

Delia was examining the books in the bookcase when Priscilla returned.

"Princess. A young man has arrived from Master Corpet with your things."

Delia brightened. "Is it allowed to have him bring them up?"

"Yes, Princess. I'll bring him here."

It didn't take long. Priscilla opened the door after a knock and Master Corpet's serving boy, Sam, came in behind her, carrying a trunk.

"Set it on the floor, Sam." Delia hurried over and clapped him on the shoulders. Sam blushed bright red. Delia had never been so happy to see a familiar face. "How are you, Sam?"

He ducked his head. "I'm fine Del… um, Princess." He looked around the room. "The whole caravan is talking." He blushed again.

"We've known each other for years, Sam. Don't be shy. Come. Sit down and have a glass of water."

He shuffled nervously to the nearest chair around the low table. Delia sat, poured him a glass of water, and handed it to him. "Please sit, Sam. Tell me what's going on?"

Priscilla moved to stand behind Delia's seat as Sam glanced at the upholstered chair, then his breeches.

"Sit, Sam. Please."

He nodded and sat, then sipped from the glass. "Uh, well news is out about you being a Princess. Master Corpet called out Emil and whipped him with his own crop, then fired him for striking you against orders. We leave tomorrow. Master is complaining that now he has no one to keep the books. He's scouring the market for a trained slave." His words tumbled from his lips in a torrent and in no particular order.

Delia found she was sad to hear that they were leaving. It was to be expected; Corpet had to be in Encre for the main slave sale. She was not sad to hear that Emil had received a come-uppance. "Isn't the Master worried that Emil will cause trouble?"

Sam shrugged. "I don't know. He doesn't seem worried. He hired another horse master and head guard to take over for Emil." He drank the water down, now that he was more relaxed. "Master Corpet has decided I should learn to read and write, now that you're gone." He beamed with pride at the announcement.

"I'm glad, Sam. You'll do well, I'm sure."

Sam rose. "I need to get back, Del… uh, Princess. Master will have a lot of packing for me to do."

Delia rose as well and threaded her arm in Sam's as she walked him to the door. "Take care, Sam, and be well. I won't forget how good a friend you've been."

He blushed again. "Thank you, Princess." He ducked his head as Priscilla led him out of the room. "You've been a good friend, too."

She waved as Priscilla shut the door. Alone, she wandered back to the window seat and stared out over the city. She'd miss Sam, but not the caravan or the men that worked it.

Delia worried a bit about Emil. He would be furious at the

whipping and being fired. He might join a brigand band and cause trouble for Master Corpet. She also worried about the word now out on the street that she was an Elven princess. That word would spread quickly and probably back to her Uncle Iyuno. How would that affect her father's war?

CHAPTER 6

The days took on a sameness, and after two months, Delia was exhausted. The magic drained her in ways she'd never thought possible. Lord Enaur was always polite but he drove her relentlessly. Today, she'd called a halt, trembling from the effort he demanded she put forth. "Enough," she'd said, sinking to the grass in the back garden. This was the spot farthest from the mansion and screened on all sides. "Safer," he'd said the second day they met. "For you and for the Trafords."

"I cannot do it."

"You can. Try again."

She shook her head. "It's not there." All she really wanted to do was lie down and sleep. Her hands lay like stones in her lap, she was so tired.

Enaur crossed his arms and took a breath, eyes closed. "Another approach, perhaps."

Delia shook her head. "Why do I need to throw fire? I can repel, shield myself, and guide my arrow to any target I can see. Isn't that enough?"

"It's not. Granted not every elf can throw fire. But your

uncle can. He'd like nothing more than to make you a target. You can make fire, so you should be able to throw it."

Idly, she'd held out her palm and concentrated. A small flame danced there, pale in the morning sunlight. She closed her hand to extinguish the flame. "It comes easily now. But throwing it seems to be beyond my skill."

"Let's try just gently tossing it. Making the flame a ball and lightly tossing."

It was two hours before she could manage to create a ball of flame. She couldn't get it to survive out of her hand. They'd stopped at mid-day and she went to her room, her whole body quivering with the morning's effort. She wolfed down the mid-day meal Priscilla brought, and once alone, tried again to create the flame ball and toss it into a small brazier she'd had Priscilla bring to the room.

She stopped at tea time when Priscilla arrived with the tea tray. "I can't seem to do it, Priscilla. Lord Enaur seems to think it's important, but I cannot do it." Delia picked up the teapot and poured a cup immediately. She hadn't realized how thirsty she'd become.

Priscilla nodded. "It must be very frustrating." The young woman thought for a moment. "When I'm learning a new thing, I'm afraid I'll fail. Then I get nervous and make a worse mess. It's not until I relax that I can master the new task. Perhaps you have the same thoughts?"

Delia put her empty cup and saucer on the tray and picked up a tiny sandwich made of cucumber and cream cheese. "Possibly. The longer I try, the more aggravated I become. I'll try again tomorrow. Clear my mind of anything else and just relax."

Priscilla put the empty tea things back on the tray and checked the pitchers of water and wine. She picked up the tray. "Shall we embroider when I return?"

"Yes." Delia smiled at Priscilla. "I've been neglecting it for magic practice. It will help me relax, take my mind off of my failure."

"Not failure, Princess. You're still learning."

After Priscilla left, Delia poured herself a goblet of white wine. Holding it, she played with making a fire in the palm of her hand. She concentrated on shaping it. First round, then square, just to see if she could. Then she tossed it up. Lightly, not very far, and practiced catching it before the little flame went out. She laughed to herself as she managed to do it once, then again and again. Laughing out loud, she was about to sip from the goblet in celebration, when the door from the hall slammed open against the wall.

Emil was there, filthy, his normally well-groomed hair and beard wild, and matted at the same time. "Bitch!"

Startled, she backed up a step.

"Thought you'd ruin me, didn't you!" He moved so fast across the room she didn't know how to react. He grabbed the goblet from her hand and drank it down, slopping wine out around his mouth and onto his already filthy shirt, then threw the goblet, back-handed, toward the fireplace. She jumped again as the silver goblet hit the stone of the fireplace and rang like a bell. It fell to the floor and circled around its base, still ringing, as Emil shouted. "That fat camel Corpet fired me because of you. And who are you anyway? Princess, my dirty beard!" That's when he slapped her.

She staggered back, hand to cheek. *Fire*, she thought, *I need to make fire*. In her panic, it wouldn't come, and Emil advanced again, pulling his crop from his belt.

"You've always thought you were better than the rest of us. Living in that wagon, protected by Corpet. Well, let's see about that. I can get good gold for you now. Word is out on the streets." He raised the crop.

That's when he began to choke. Emil's free hand went to his throat. When he began to foam around the mouth, he dropped the crop and put the second hand to his face.

What was happening? He dropped to his knees. She was more scared now than when he was advancing on her.

A horrible noise came from him. A sound like the time one of the caravan horses had broken a leg. It was heart-rending and worse than if he had screamed. He fell over on his right side, nails clawing at his throat. Unbidden, his aura came to her. It was brown and gray and the sparkles were rapidly diminishing. She took a step toward him but she didn't know what to do. Worse, he began to convulse just as Priscilla returned.

She turned and ran out of the room, leaving the door open.

Delia sank down onto the window seat, Emil's death happening right in front of her. Finally. Blessedly, he stopped moving. The horrific noise bled to a stop. She was shaking when the house guards came bursting into her room, Priscilla right behind them.

"Princess!" Priscilla called out. She danced around the guards as they surrounded the now still man on the floor. "Are you all right?"

Delia raised a shaking hand. "I, I think so. Yes. I'm fine."

"No, you're not." Priscilla reached out to Delia's face. "The animal struck you!"

"I'm fine." She stopped staring at Emil and looked at Priscilla. "He drank the wine."

After that, the house was in an uproar. That evening she was called down to Lord Traford's den. Lord Enaur and Sir Alexis were there. The younger man poured her a glass of sherry, and she sat with it in one of the smaller chairs.

"We've deduced what happened," Lord Traford began. He

sipped a brown liquid from a squat, heavy glass, then continued. "The man who attacked you was fired from Corpet's caravan. You knew that, I hear."

Delia nodded, then sipped her sherry. Her hand trembled. She was never, ever, going to get his dying sounds out of her head.

"Well," the Lord shook his head. "He decided to take up with the criminals in the city. His claim to you that he was going to sell you was true." He looked sadly at Enaur. "Despite my best efforts, everyone in the city seems to know you are here."

"Worse," Enaur broke in. "There's a bounty for you. One lord or another bidding ever higher for you. And not just here in Katzin. All around the country."

"What do we do?" Delia asked. Since this afternoon she'd been a wreck. The threat Traford and Enaur had told her of was now more than real.

"We keep doing what we're doing," Enaur said with a deep sigh. "You need to be trained before we leave the safety of the Lord's palace."

Delia was having difficulty with the attack. "How did he get in?"

"One of the new stable hands," Sir Alexis said. He sounded so disgusted that Delia looked up from her drink. "He let the dastard into the yard and the stable hand's new girlfriend let him into the house."

"My sincere apologies, Princess," Lord Traford broke in. "The two have been fired and escorted from the city."

Worse and worse, Delia thought. *That poor housemaid. The poor stable hand.* Where would they go? What would they do? Katzin was scores of miles across the desert from the next city.

Her face must have shown her feelings. Lord Enaur

spoke. "Do not worry about them, Princess. They had already sold you to Emil."

She nodded. Of course. But how awful. They would die out in the desert. "And the wine?"

"I checked what was in the ewer, Princess," Enaur said. "Poisoned."

All she could do was shake her head. "But not by Emil. He couldn't have known it was poisoned. He drank it."

"True." Lord Traford nodded. "We followed the wine in its journey to your room. We questioned Priscilla first."

A shock of fear went through Delia. "Is she sound?" The thought that Priscilla would be harmed, or worse, be involved, was just too much to bear.

"She's fine," Sir Alexis said. "She was very helpful."

"Priscilla went to the kitchen and asked one of the scullery maids for a ewer as she was preparing your lunch. She poured the wine from the cask herself. So as far as we can tell, the ewer was poisoned, not the wine itself." Lord Traford sat back in his leather armchair and sipped his drink.

"But, what about the scullery maid?" Delia was imagining bodies lined up in a row. *First Emil, then the maid and the stable hand, now this girl.*

"She disappeared," Enaur told her. When I and Lord Traford and Alexis went to the kitchens, no one had seen the girl in hours."

"Oh dear. Why would the girl do that?"

"Payment, most likely," Enaur said. He sighed. "A shame. We would have liked to have spoken to her."

Delia wondered how desperate these people were that they would sell out to Emil. Or to the poisoner. "No one else was hurt, were they?"

"You mean, no one else was poisoned?" Traford asked. "No. No one else. A bad business, this. Very bad."

"We'll stay until I'm satisfied that the Princess can defend herself. Then we'll go," Enaur said.

"Well enough," Traford said. "Well enough."

The next day Delia did what she'd promised Priscilla the day before. Putting aside her little victory of tossing the ball of fire up and catching it, she emptied her mind of everything but the fire. She focused on drawing the flame and shaping it into a ball and like a child's ball, she tossed it. It flew three feet before winking out in the damp grass. Delia crowed with joy. "I did it. I did it!"

Enaur, grinned at her. "So I see, Princess. Well done. Let's practice more."

With one success, Delia was more confident, and worked all morning at throwing the flame ball farther and farther. By mid-day, she could throw it thirty feet and set the target on fire.

"Well done, Princess." Enaur snuffed the fire out with his magic and faced the princess. "I think it's time to travel to your father."

Delia's eyes went wide. "So soon?"

"We can practice more on the way, but yes. I've received word that your great-uncle is readying a large force. It's time."

She nodded. "When?"

"It will take a few days to prepare."

"Very well." Delia pulled herself erect. She didn't know how she felt about leaving. The mansion was beginning to feel like home. "I suppose the Trafords will be glad to have us gone. We've been here a long time."

He chuckled. "Lord Traford derives a great deal of status by having elves stay with him. He doesn't mind at all." The two began the walk back to the house. "I'll arrange for horses and two elf guards, and supplies, of course. You should have riding attire made. I know where to find an elf dress-maker who will know what to do."

"Thank you." Delia wondered if elf clothing was very different from human clothing. "What should I bring?"

"Anything that will fit into your saddle bags. We won't have a baggage train."

"Hard riding then? I'm afraid I'm not a good horse-woman. I usually rode in my wagon."

"You'll adapt."

They parted ways at the conservatory. "Five days, I think, to prepare." Lord Enaur bowed and left.

Delia went to her room and looked through the trunk Sam had brought her. It contained mostly clothing, nothing fine except a silk scarf she'd bought at a market. Blue silk, the color of her eyes. She'd keep that. Everything else could be thrown away. She picked up the handkerchief in the embroidery hoop that was on the window seat. There wouldn't be room for fine threads and needles in her saddle bags. Delia sat down and worked on the piece. It should at least be finished before she left.

The afternoon was broken by the arrival of the elven dress-maker. Everything was moving fast, Delia thought as the woman measured and showed her sketches. Too fast.

CHAPTER 7

The preparations went quickly, and on the morning of her departure, Delia had said good-bye to Priscilla at breakfast.

"You've been wonderful, Priscilla. Thank you." She handed the maid a tiny, paper-wrapped package. "Open it."

Priscilla nodded and carefully unwrapped the gift. "Your handkerchief! I can't." She tried to hand it back. "You worked so hard on it."

"You keep it. You gave me the gift of teaching me how to embroider. The least I can do is give you my first, although not very good, effort."

"It's beautiful. You did wonderful work on it."

"You're nice to say so, Priscilla. Thank you. But keep it. I'm sure I can find needle and thread with the elves and make more." With that she gave the maid a hug. "I'll miss you."

"I'll miss you as well, Princess."

Now the Trafords were at the stables to say good-bye. Delia hugged Lady Traford and shook hands with Sir Alexis and Lord Traford. "Thank you all for allowing me to stay so long. You've been lovely and gracious hosts."

"Nonsense, Princess," Lady Traford responded. "You are a delightful guest. We're very happy to have you back any time."

Lord Enaur mounted his horse. The two other elves were already mounted. "Time to leave, Princess." He nodded to Lord Traford. "I'll send word when we arrive. I have your messages to the king."

Lord Traford nodded as Delia mounted. "Thank you, Lord Enaur. You're welcome here any time."

The elves wheeled their horses around and waved.

"Safe travels," Lady Traford called out.

Delia waved and followed Enaur. The other two elves followed her.

It didn't take long to be outside of Katzin. Delia rode beside Enaur. "Do you think we'll have trouble along the road?"

"It's possible. Your uncle has had weeks to move his people into place to find you. Nothing is a secret for long."

Delia turned in the saddle to the elves riding behind her. "What are your names?"

The elf on her right bowed from the saddle. "Sachi Arako, Princess."

The elf on her left also bowed. "Kiri Dan'os, Princess."

"Their families are loyal to your father, Princess."

Delia nodded to the two and turned back around in her saddle. "How long to get there?"

"A week, Princess. I've cast a glamour on us, making us hard to see. But of course, to other elves, we are detectable. I'm planning on speed to get us there more than magic. We can hope that speed will be enough."

Delia nodded. It had only been an hour and she was already feeling the pain begin in her thighs. It was going to be a long trip.

They'd been six days on the road without incident. Delia was looking forward to arriving at the castle today. A hot bath would be welcome. She had worried about meeting her parents as she saddled the horse at dawn. What did they look like? Would they appear old or young, like Enaur? How should she greet them? Bow? Hug? She had no idea.

The morning passed uneventfully, and they dismounted at a stream to water the horses. Delia chewed on a piece of jerky as she held her horse's reins while it drank in the middle of the shallow stream. The day was warm and the sound of the water dancing over the stones in the stream was soothing. She was half dozing when an arrow whizzed by her head and thunked into the stream bank. Her head came up, and wide-eyed, she looked around.

"Mount. Mount up!" Enaur cried out as he leapt into his saddle. "Ride!"

Delia dropped the jerky and scrambled into her saddle, the horse dancing in the stream in confusion at the commotion. In the saddle finally, she wheeled the horse around as more arrows whizzed by. She kicked the beast in the sides and scrambled up the bank after Enaur. Sachi and Kiri were right behind her.

Kiri cried out in pain. Delia turned to look. "Run, Princess. Don't wait. Ride! Ride!"

She saw Sachi help Kiri so she kicked the horse again. It sprang forward—nearly unseating her—after Enaur.

"We're almost there. Ride, Princess!"

The two raced along the road, Delia glancing back for Kiri and Sachi. "Kiri was hurt!"

"Can't be helped right now, Princess." Arrows thudded into the ground on either side of them.

"I don't see anyone," she called out.

"They've covered themselves in a glamour. Can you throw a fire ball behind us?"

Delia had all she could do to hang on. She didn't think she could turn around and throw a fire ball with the horse at full gallop. "I don't know."

"Try, Princess."

She let go of the saddle horn with her right hand and twisted a little in the saddle. She didn't see anyone there until another arrow flew by her head. There, in the middle of the road, a glimmer. Delia gathered her focus and in almost one motion created a ball of fire and threw it directly behind her.

A horse screamed, then the glamour collapsed. There were six riders behind them, gaining ground. She kicked her horse again, threw another fireball and missed. The riders spread out.

"We're almost there," Enaur called.

Delia took a look ahead. She didn't see anything. "Is it also glamoured?"

"Yes. They'll see the fight and come out to us."

She threw another fireball at the lead rider. It hit the horse in the chest. It reared, screaming, and dumped the rider in the dirt.

The sound of horns came from ahead of her. She turned to look. There, a castle wall appeared, and a gate was opening. A column of riders came out and broke around them as they pursued the attackers. Enaur and Delia raced through the gates. The horses came to a stop, breathing heavily and covered with sweat. Elves ran to them and helped them down. Delia watched the gate; no attackers came through. She realized she was shaking.

"We're safe, Princess."

"What about Kiri and Sachi?"

"Our people will find them."

Delia looked around her. This was no ordinary castle. It was made of stone but in form, it was light and delicate. A fountain burbled in the center of this courtyard, and trees and flowers grew around the edges. "Is it all like this?"

Enaur smiled. "Better. This is a work space, so less decorated."

An elf came and took the horses' reins. "Come, Princess. We'll get you settled. We meet your parents before dinner."

Delia shuddered. The thing she'd most hoped for was finally coming true. She wasn't sure how she felt about it.

CHAPTER 8

Delia stood outside her parent's private rooms, staring at the door. Her escort, Lord Enaur, had just knocked on it. As the door opened, she ran her sweaty palms down the skirt of the dress she'd been given.

There stood a female elf, her golden hair braided and put up around her head like a crown. She was simply dressed in a sky-blue gown, embroidered with silver in leaves and vines. She was stunning. A wide smile spread across her face. "Delia!" She opened her arms and wrapped them around Delia in a warm embrace. "I'm so glad you're finally home."

Delia had never felt more welcome anywhere before. Love seemed to flow from her mother like a warm blanket. "Mother."

Ralae let Delia go and stepped back to look at her. "You look wonderful. So lovely. Come, meet your father." She threaded her arm in Delia's and escorted her into the room. "You as well, Enaur."

They proceeded into the room where intricately woven carpets covered the stone floors. There was a huge fireplace on the opposite wall and a desk under a window. The elf seated there turned around and stood up. His hair was so blond it was nearly white and hung down loose over his shoulders. Dressed in a green tunic with gold embroidery and black trousers tucked into boots that rose to his knees, he met them half way across the floor, next to a dining table and chairs. He took Delia by the shoulders, his face solemn. "We've missed you terribly, Delia. Can you ever forgive us?" He embraced her.

Delia chose to look at his aura; it was silver, sparkling. She could feel his power and sadness and grief, and hugged him back. "I understand it was something you felt needed to be done."

He released her and stepped back. Looking at her, then Lord Enaur. "You arrived in a rush."

Enaur nodded. "They ambushed us at the stream. Kiri and Sachi?"

Ucheni sighed. "They were both injured, they're with the mage now, healing. I'm sorry about the attack. They hid well, as I had ordered the approaches to be swept just this morning."

"We're all safe. that's what matters," Enaur said.

Ralae walked to the upholstered chairs in front of the fireplace. "Come, sit down. Tell us about you, Delia. We want to know everything."

They talked for two hours, telling each other about their lives, the war, and her training.

"Delia has a gift, Sire, for languages and writing, but she has the strength to throw fireballs and is very accurate with them."

The king and queen smiled. "That's good to hear. We have so few with the power to do that. It will be a great help in the war."

Ralae stood up. "It's time for dinner. We can go down

together. Everyone is eager to meet you. There will be a feast and music all night to welcome you." She took Delia by the hand. "I never want to let you go again."

The banquet was set up in a hall on the main floor of the palace. Delia had never seen anything like it. Sconces attached to the wall and chandeliers hanging from the ceiling were lit with glowing orbs casting a soft clear light over everything. They were like magic to Delia. Massive tapestries worked in brilliant colors hung on the dressed stone walls. Long tables filled the room. Elves stood beside them, wine cups in hand, waiting.

They cheered when Ucheni on one side and Ralae on the other, escorted Delia between them to the head table. Delia blushed at the overwhelming wash of love and welcome that flowed in her direction. Ucheni raised his hands and the crowd quieted. "Thank you for your warm welcome to our daughter, Princess Delia. Please, let us enjoy this feast."

Another cheer went up as everyone claimed a seat. A group of musicians played, people sang. She hardly remembered what she ate as one person after another came to the table to greet her. After the banquet, there was dancing and one young male elf after another took turns teaching her to dance. Her parents joined her on the dance floor and the hours passed so quickly she hardly realized dawn was breaking.

She stood beside her parents as each elf took their leave. Delia was enjoying looking at everyone's aura. They were in every color she'd ever heard of and all who said their good nights were full of good wishes. She was shocked, then, by one of the last elves to make a farewell. An elf with age etched on his face, he was dressed all in black, the only one in that color.

Her father spoke. "Lord Nethene, my daughter, Delia."

The blackness of his aura caused Delia to shudder as he bent over her hand. "I'm so glad you've finally returned home."

Delia took her hand back as fast as she could. "Lord Nethene."

He studied her, a smirk on his face. Was he reading her aura as well? "We all look forward to your help in this unfortunate war."

"I'll do what I can." She could feel her skin crawling. Didn't her parents feel it?

Nethene left and Delia trembled with relief. She barely heard the last of the guests speaking to her.

Alone, her mother took her arm. "I'll lead you to your room, Sweetness. Did you have a good time?"

Ucheni walked with them.

"I did, until just now."

Ucheni's eyebrows rose. "Just now?"

"Yes. Couldn't you feel Lord Nethene's aura? It was black as a well bottom. He is evil."

Her parents looked at each other. "His aura is purple, Delia. He's a distant cousin on your mother's side of the family. Are you sure?"

Her nod was emphatic. "I could hardly stand for him to touch my hand." She shuddered. "Can an aura be masked? Hidden?"

Ralae shook her head. "I've never heard of that. But perhaps the mages will know."

They reached her room. "I'll ask in the morning," Ucheni said.

Delia nodded. "Thank you."

Her parents nodded. "Sleep well," Ralae told her.

"You as well." Delia experimented. "Mother. Father." The words didn't feel natural. She closed the door and leaned against it. She had a horrible feeling about Lord Nethene that just wouldn't go away.

She splashed her face and dressed for bed, throwing the bolt on the door before she lay down. Everyone in the palace would know where she was and she didn't want Nethene sneaking in.

CHAPTER 9

D elia was called to the king's office, a room off of his private bedroom, at midmorning. There she found King Ucheni, Queen Ralae, Lord Enaur and an elf stranger. He was dressed in dark purple robes, his white hair cut just to his shoulders and waving wildly around his head. They all turned as she entered.

"Mage Kaepli, this is my daughter, Delia."

Delia stepped forward to shake his hand. "Sir. I'm so sorry we didn't meet last night."

"Happy to meet you at last, Your Highness. I was caring for your friends, Sachi and Kiri. They're doing well. They'll be up and around in no time."

"That's good to hear." She looked to her father. "You asked him about masking auras?"

"Please, sit, everyone." He sat down at his desk. "Kaepli, please proceed."

Kaepli steepled his fingers. "I had to look long and hard this morning, Sire. But at the end, it is possible." He turned to Delia, seated next to him. "You say you see his aura as black?"

She nodded. "As a moonless, cloudy night. But Father says he sees Nethene's aura as purple. Is that what you see as well?"

The old elf nodded. "Indeed." He sighed. "It takes great power to mask your own aura and it has to be held day and night. At least to people you don't want to know. I didn't know Nethene had such power."

"I felt a great evil from him." She looked at King Ucheni. "You say he's a relative. Any indication of evil from him before? Is he a supporter of yours?"

Lord Enaur spoke first. "I've never heard him speak of anything but support for His Majesty. I've never heard him say anything about Iyuno at all."

"Daughter," Queen Ralae spoke. "He's a distant cousin whom I only saw a few times as I was growing up. He joined us here when Iyuno declared war." She looked at Mage Kaepli. "There was no rumor at all of him being powerful enough to mask an aura."

"He's always given good advice at council." King Ucheni tapped his fingertips on the carved wooden arm of his chair. "This is very disturbing. I am thinking back over the years. Is it possible he's informing for Iyuno?"

"That's quite a leap, Sire." Lord Enaur's eyebrows rose. "Do you have something in mind?"

The king shrugged. "I don't know. We'd have to review every decision we've made while Nethene was in council, and any correlating failures afterward."

"There are records, Sire." Kaepli stroked the skirt of his robe. "I could have two or three of my students search them."

Ucheni drew a deep breath. "Yes. Do that. I need to be sure we don't have a spy among us." He stood up, then the others did as well. "Thank you for coming. Kaepli, could you stay a moment?"

"Certainly." He bowed as the others left for the door.

Out in the hall, Ralae threaded her arm through Delia's as Enaur went the other way down the hall. "Why were you looking at auras, daughter?"

Delia shrugged. "They're new to me. They're so pretty and so many different colors. Nethene's was so... so violent. Evil." She shuddered at the memory.

"Kaepli and your father will sort it all out. In the meantime, would you like a tour of the palace and the grounds?"

"That would be wonderful." Delia broke into a grin.

It was two days before Delia was called back to her father's office. Her mother, the king, the mage and Enaur were already there. "You found something?"

King Ucheni motioned to the mage to go ahead.

"In a significant number of cases, there is a correlation between an action taken by the council, only to have it fail when executed. For every failure, Nethene was at the Council meeting."

Enaur pounded the arm of his chair. "No wonder we're not winning."

"Calm, My Lord." The king raised his hand. "Let's think this through. How might we use this to our advantage?"

Delia blinked. "Sire. You mean to keep him here? A traitor?"

Ucheni folded his hands in front of him on the desk. "A real possibility. We could feed him false information. It would have to be handled delicately. An elf with power enough to mask his aura may very well have other powers we know nothing about." He looked at Ralae. "Have you heard anything about his magical strength?"

"I sent word to various cousins, aunts and uncles. My mother, as well. But it will be days before the messengers can get to their homes, then return." She sighed.

"In the meantime, I suggest," the king continued, "that we not let him know we suspect him."

"Won't our auras give us away?" Delia thought this was a terrible idea.

"They will indicate we're hiding something," the mage said. "But except for newly fledged elves, no one really goes around studying everyone else's auras."

Everyone else nodded, but Delia wasn't convinced. There was nothing she could do about it though. There was a short discussion on how to work the council meetings when Nethene was present, then the meeting disbanded. Delia went to the armory.

She asked for a bow and arrows and went to the practice ground. There, other elves were target shooting. They nodded their acknowledgment of her, then left her to her own practice. She stayed there two hours, her arm trembling at the end. She returned the bow and arrows to the armory then went to her room, throwing the bolt when she closed the door.

Delia paced until the sun began to set, with no new ideas. She was going to have to go along with her father's plan. But she intended to be there armed. Just in case.

CHAPTER 10

Delia sat behind her father at the council meeting, three days after they'd decided to keep Lord Nethene in place. Mage Kaepli was on the king's right, Lord Enaur on his left. Lord Nethene sat two chairs down from the king, next to Ecaur. The Guard Captain, Neoni, sat next to Nethene, and next to the Mage sat the Chief of Scouts, Mysteso. Mysteso was telling the council about the movements of Iyuno's forces. The news wasn't good.

"They're massing, Sire, two day's ride from here in the Diamond Point valley. I dare say there will be a challenge issued soon."

King Ucheni nodded. "Captain Neoni, how are your forces prepared?"

"I've been recalling squads for the last week, Sire. Most are back. I've only kept a few watchers on key passes and routes. We can march in an hour, if you feel the need."

"It seems prudent, Sire," Nethene steepled his fingers, "to send your forces to Iyuno's battleground immediately."

Delia watched her uncle closely. Something about his tone of voice made the hairs on her arms stand straight up.

"Not wait for the challenge?" Mysteso asked.

Nethene shook his head. "If you arrive before the challenge, Iyuno will know that you've been watching him. That you're not surprised."

Nethene's aura was black as night, Delia saw when she shifted her gaze to her magical sight. She clasped her hands in her lap to keep them from twisting. She didn't trust Nethene, and thought his plan to send all of her father's soldiers to Diamond Point Valley dangerous. It could be a trap, or a diversion. She nodded when Neoni said just that.

Nethene glanced at her over the king's shoulder. She shuddered at his gaze and felt as though he knew exactly what she was thinking. Delia felt for the knife she'd taken to wearing at her waist. It slid easily a fraction of an inch from the sheath. That made her feel a little better. If the evil elf decided to do anything, she was ready.

Mage Kaepli tapped the table in front of him. "I agree, Neoni. We don't know if these massed troops are his entire force or a diversion. Attack could come from any direction."

"Have you done a scrying, Kaepli?" the king asked.

"Not yet, Sire." The old mage bowed his head to the king. "But now seems the right time. I'll prepare as soon as the council is finished."

Ucheni nodded. "Good. I'll await your word. That will be all for today."

There was much scraping of chairs away from the table and bowing to the king. Delia caught Nethene glancing at her as he bowed, a look that to her meant he knew what she was thinking. A shiver ran down her spine and her left hand began forming a fireball of its own accord. She saw him restrain a smile as he turned to leave the council hall. She stood behind her father, ready to burn the elf down if needed.

Kaepli raised an eyebrow as he saw her behind the king. "Delia?"

Ucheni turned in his seat to stare at her. "What's wrong, daughter?"

Nethene left the room. Delia breathed easier. "It was the way he looked at me, Father. My hand began to form a fireball without my conscious thought."

Ucheni raised an eyebrow, then looked at the mage. "Is that possible?"

"Apparently. I just saw her do it. You were that afraid?"

Delia nodded. Her hands were trembling. "I don't trust a thing he said, Father. It's either a trap or a decoy."

"You don't think Iyuno will send a challenge to meet in Diamond Point Valley?"

"I do think he will, but I don't think he'll be there. He'll be attacking the castle or ambush you on your way."

The mage stroked his chin. "That could be true, Sire." He took a deep breath. "Let me see what the scrying bowl says. That should help guide your decision."

The king nodded and the mage hurried off. Ucheni turned to his daughter. "Are you well?"

She took a deep breath. "A little terrified. I'll recover." Delia wiped her hand on her skirt.

He took her by the shoulders. "I worry that all of this is too overwhelming for you."

"I'll be fine, Father." She raised her chin and looked him in the eyes. "I barely found you. I don't want to lose you just yet."

He gave her a hug. "I've never had a more enthusiastic defender."

"I'll do my best."

Back in her room, Delia changed into work clothes and went to the practice ground. She found a spot away from the others and began to throw fireballs. The other elves gathered around to watch. She practiced throwing far, then for accuracy. She answered questions about how she was forming the balls as best she could. Several of the elves began to try it. A few managed small fires in their hands but not the fire she could achieve.

She was able to spar with one or two of the elves with staves, a weapon she had the least skill with but one she felt she should at least have a basic grasp of. No one could tell what would or could go wrong in a battle. Delia was worried about that. Being the bookkeeper on a caravan hardly prepared her for going into a war. She wasn't sure how she'd react. She thanked the elves for teaching her the staves and went back to her room.

As she washed in the cold water in her basin, Delia spent more time worrying about Nethene. Could he see her aura color with fear? Probably. She wondered if she could mask her aura. *How* to mask it was the first question. She looked in the polished silver of her mirror. Her aura was green with sparkles. Delia thought hard, pulling energy from her core, to change the color of her aura. It didn't change at all, as far as she could tell. She gave it up as a waste of time. Perhaps Kaepli would know how. She resolved to ask him at dinner. It would be handy to be able to hide what she was feeling from Nethene.

CHAPTER 11

Nethene sat three elves away from Delia at dinner. As family, he rated a seat at the head table, but that didn't make her happy about it. Her venison lay cold on the plate as she worried about what her distant cousin might do.

Mage Kaepli sat beside her father. Delia could hear enough of their conversation past her mother to know they were discussing the scrying Kaepli had finished. "Confusion," she'd overheard him say. That didn't sound good to her. She wished she had more experience. It was a handicap of immense proportions that she had been separated from her people and from magic for so long. Her hand began to tingle as fire began to form. Delia squashed the urge and shook out her hand under the table.

At the rear of the hall the musicians warmed up. Dinner was nearly over and she was anxious to talk to the Mage about how to mask her aura. She saw her chance as the Mage rose to take his leave of the king and queen. She rose as well. "If you don't mind, Father, Mother, I'd like to retire. I'm afraid I overdid it on the practice field today."

Her mother nodded. "Of course, Sweetheart."

Delia leaned down to kiss her mother on the cheek. "Thank you, Mother. Enjoy the music." She walked around her mother's chair to the king. She kissed him on the cheek as well. "Good evening, Father."

He patted her hand. "Sleep well, Delia."

She saw Nethene watching and a tingle of fear ran down her spine. "Thank you, Father." She turned to the Mage. "May I walk with you, Kaepli?"

"Of course, Princess." He bowed and let her go first.

Delia could feel Nethene watching her until they left the hall. "I have a question."

Kaepli nodded. "I suspected. Go on."

"How does Nethene mask his aura?"

The mage drew a deep breath. "The books say it has to do with the control of your core. Which begs the question, of course." He shook his head. "The text talks about your essence, which is the core, of course, and focus." Kaepli waved a hand. "All magic requires focus, so that is less than helpful."

"May I read the texts?"

The old mage's eyebrow rose. "An unusual request, but I don't see why not. Come by my workshop in the morning. I'll have the books ready for you."

She was disappointed. She wanted to read them now. "Not tonight?"

The mage shook his head. "My apologies, Princess, but the texts are scattered. Let me and my apprentices find them all and set aside a table for you. It will go much faster that way."

Delia swallowed her impatience. "Of course. In the morning then."

Kaepli stopped at the hall leading to the wing where his

workshops were and bowed. "In the morning. Sleep well, Princess."

She bowed in return and continued on to her rooms. After bolting the door, she prepared for bed, but was too restless to lie down. As she paced, she absent-mindedly formed fireballs, tossing them from one hand to another, then putting them out. Then she realized she was making them in multiples, not just one at a time. That piqued her interest and at the fireplace, focused on making as many at a time as she could.

By midnight she was drained, physically and mentally. She let the fireballs expire and washed her hands and face in the basin then lay down. Her last thoughts were of auras.

In the morning she hardly spared time to eat the bread, fruit and cheese brought to her room. She hurried to the mage's workshop and stopped just inside the door. She saw a large room, herbs hanging from the ceiling, several heavy wooden tables with stools at them. Some had apprentices already working. Books and scrolls filled the shelves that lined the walls. She cleared her throat.

An apprentice looked up from a huge tome he was reading. "Your Highness!" He jumped from his stool and came to her. "Welcome. Mage Kaepli directed me to assist you. I'm Sisruo. Come right this way."

A handsome elf, she thought as he led her to a table under a window. He brought her to a stool next to the table where six leather-bound books were stacked to one side. "We found these for you. The pages with the information you wanted are book-marked. If you have any questions, please let me know."

Delia nodded. Everything seemed well organized. She admired his hair, he'd cut it so that it ended at his jaw. She pulled her thoughts away from his jawline. "Thank you. I won't keep you from your work. Where is Mage Kaepli?"

"He's gone to a glade, Princess. To try the scrying again."

She was disappointed. She'd hoped to talk to him about what she was about to read. "Oh. Very well."

"May I get you some water?"

"That would be nice. Yes. Thank you, Sisuro. Have you been an apprentice long?"

"Long enough. I test for my mage status soon."

"Congratulations." She climbed onto the stool. "Sorry for keeping you."

"I'm happy to assist you, Princess. I'll let you get to your research." He turned and left.

Delia looked at the stack of books. The largest was on the bottom with the books getting smaller toward the top of the stack. She pulled the smallest book to her and opened the cover. The writing was in a flowing script, the book title so elaborate it was difficult to read. Delia turned a few pages to find treatises on the essence of the core, how to force plant growth, and one on changing hair color. There didn't seem to be any overall theme to the book, just whatever the author had decided to write about. She found the bookmark and flipped to the page. This treatise was titled, "Auras and Their Control." That sounded promising.

Sisruo returned and placed a tray with a pitcher of water and a mug on her table. "Princess."

She looked up from the page and smiled. "Thank you, Sisruo."

He bowed. "Ask if you need anything."

"I will. Thank you."

He left and she watched him go back to his table before she went back to the page. With luck, she'd learn everything she needed to know from this one book.

CHAPTER 12

Delia rubbed her eyes then arched backwards to relieve the strain in her back from leaning over the table for hours. When she looked around, she realized that all of the apprentices were gone. She'd been so engrossed with the books that she hadn't heard anyone come or go. The door opened and Sisruo entered with a tray. He came to her table.

"Good, you're taking a break." He placed the tray in an open spot on her table.

Delia's stomach growled in reply. She blushed.

Sisruo chuckled. "Studying is hard work, Princess. No shame in that."

"I didn't hear anyone leave."

"We practice moving quietly. There's usually someone studying or doing research and we don't want to disturb them."

"Very polite." Delia glanced at the tray. "There's enough here for three people. Will you join me?"

"I'd love to." He walked to the next table and brought over a stool while Delia moved books to one side of her workspace.

He pulled the tray over to sit between them. "I took the liberty of bringing wine to have with our mid-day meal. I can get more water, if you'd prefer."

"A little wine sounds nice." She reached for her water mug, drank the rest of it, then put it back on the table.

Sisuro poured for her then poured a little into a second cup. He handed her a plate and a napkin then took one for himself. "You pick first, Princess."

She selected an apple, some yellow cheese and a small loaf of bread. "I'm afraid I didn't eat much breakfast this morning."

"Understandable." He took a loaf, a pear and some white cheese. "I get that way myself when I have something I'm eager to study." He ripped off a chunk of the loaf and with his belt knife, took a slice of pear and another of cheese to make a bite. "What have you discovered?" He ate his bite.

Delia used her knife to slice up her apple, then the cheese. She wiped her blade on the napkin. "Much of each article was in language so vague as to be worthless. It's as though the author wanted to brag about knowing or finding something but wasn't willing to share the actual information." She shook her head as she ate the apple, bread and cheese bite.

Sisruo nodded. "That happens a lot. We've learned to read around the flowery, bragging language and figure out what they are saying. But what did you learn that was concrete?"

"Over and over, each text said it was a matter of core control." She took a sip of wine. It was a white with a bright, fruity flavor. "As Mage Kaepli said last night, that's pretty standard for magic. Book four," she pointed at a medium-sized leather-bound book to her left, "had more specific instruction. Not just a matter of our core, but our essence is needed to change one's aura." She studied Sisruo. "Do you understand what it may mean, our essence?"

The apprentice took a deep breath and finished his mouthful. "Not the core, but who you are. Deep inside, when things go bad, when no one's looking, the part of you that's the most real." He shook his head. "Your soul, perhaps is the shortest description I can give."

Delia's eyebrows drew together. She'd been in many a situation over the years that was bad. How had she reacted? Was she ever mean? She didn't think so. Indifferent? Possibly, given her own situation. Probably, more like it. Suddenly, every mean thing she'd ever done, said, or even thought, popped into her mind. She instantly felt guilty and ashamed. A blush crept up her cheeks.

"Stop that."

Startled, Delia nearly dropped her cup. She looked up at Sisruo.

"You're imagining great personal crimes when in reality you were just being normal."

"How…?"

He snorted. "It's part of our training to look into our own souls and understand who we are. We can't become a full mage until we do." He looked down at his plate. "I've been there, so I recognized it when you were going through it."

She sighed. Now she felt like an idiot. "There's so much I don't know."

"True, but all it takes is training." He ate another bite of bread as she nibbled an apple slice.

They sat, each in their own thoughts for a few moments.

"Can you teach me?" she said finally.

"You want to be an apprentice?" He looked surprised.

"No, not that. I'm trying to change the color of my aura as other people see it. If knowing my own soul is what has to happen to allow me to do this, then that's what I must do."

Sisruo frowned at his plate. "Master Kaepli knows what you're doing?"

"Yes." Delia wiped her hands and put the napkin on the table. "Where do we begin?"

He took a last bite of pear then a sip of wine and put his napkin down. "Fine." He focused on her. "Ah, green with sparkles."

She nodded. "And yours is," she smiled, "blue with gold swirls. Pretty!"

Sisruo chuckled. "Your's too." The smile left his face. "Why do you want to mask your aura?"

"I don't, necessarily. I want to know how someone else would do it. Also, it would be helpful, at times, if I could hide my true feelings from others."

The apprentice tugged at an earlobe.

She wondered if she'd broken some convention. He nodded, slowly. "I can see where that would be an advantage. Hide your glee, or fear, or knowledge. Yes. Useful." He nodded again. "Fine. Let's look at your soul. Tell me what you were thinking earlier."

Three hours later, Kaepli found them still on the stools, staring at each other. "Sisruo?"

The apprentice came out of the study first. "Master." He blinked and took a deep breath.

Delia followed. She was dazed and overwhelmingly thirsty. She grabbed her cup and drank down the wine. A sigh escaped her lips as reality came back to her. "We were looking at my soul, Mage Kaepli."

Kaepli's bushy eyebrows rose. "So you found something?"

"A little something." She poured the last of the water in the pitcher into her cup and drank it all. "It needs my core and an understanding of who I am."

Kaepli turned to Sisruo. "And you found?"

"We can both change our auras, at least a little and for a short time. It's very difficult to achieve and even harder to hold." He slid off of his stool. "Please, Master, sit. You must be tired from the scrying."

The old elf waved his hand. "I'm not that decrepit, youngling." He eyed the pitcher on the tray of food. "Is any wine left?"

The apprentice nodded. "Certainly." He poured some into the third cup and handed it over. "Can you tell us your news?"

The mage sat on the vacated stool. "Yes. I should."

CHAPTER 13

K aepli settled with a sigh and sipped the wine, setting the cup down before beginning. "It's confusion in the scrying bowl. I suspect Nethene or Iyuno or both, are interfering." He sipped more wine as he stroked his beard. "I did see some flashes of an army massing. It could have been Diamond Point Valley, but the reading was too muddled. There were other quick views, a forest, but I couldn't tell where, and a lake." He pulled at an earlobe. "The lake could have been anywhere, but there were several large boats, suitable to carry soldiers." Kaepli shook his head and pulled a bit of bread off of Sisruo's leftover loaf. He chewed slowly. "No. It just wasn't clear enough to make heads or tails of it." He stood up. "I must tell the king."

"Shall I accompany you?" Delia slid from her stool. "I think I've done all I can here today."

Master Kaepli nodded. "I'd be honored, Princess."

Delia blushed. It was hard to accept the title still. She turned to Sisruo. "Thank you for your help today. May I return tomorrow to practice?" *Say yes*, she thought to herself. *Say yes!*

He bowed. "I'd be honored."

The mage clapped his hands. "Good. We'll go to the king. Sisruo, make notes about what you've done today. We might as well keep a good record."

"Yes, Master Kaepli. Immediately."

Kaepli and Delia left. She glanced behind her as she followed the mage through the door. Sisuro was watching. He smiled. She gave him a tiny wave and closed the door. Her eyes were on the ground, a smile on her face when Kaepli broke into her thoughts.

"You and Sisruo worked well together today?"

She shook her thoughts clear. "Yes, Mage Kaepli. He had everything prepared for me and made sure I didn't die of hunger or thirst while I worked. A very thoughtful elf. He told me he's nearly ready for his last tests."

The old elf nodded. "He's been ready for a while now. He just lacks the confidence. But he'll get there." Kaepli glanced at Delia. "And your study? How long can you hold the changed aura?"

"Not long, which is frustrating. I have to focus so hard, it's exhausting."

"Interesting, then, that Nethene can hold it for so long. I do wonder why you see through it and no one else can?"

"I've wondered that as well. The prophecy says I'm the most powerful, so that might explain it. It doesn't explain why I can't hold my own false aura."

"Practice." The old elf opened the door to the hall for her. "Power is one thing, skill something else. You'll get it."

She nodded. Once in the king's office, the mage told him everything he'd told her and his apprentice. King Ucheni sighed and leaned back in his chair. "We'll have to send scouts. You have no idea where the woods or the lake are?"

"No Sire. I think the council should be involved. Especially Chief of Scouts Mysteso and Captain Neoni."

Ucheni's eyebrow raised. "Not Nethene?"

"I'd advise not, Sire."

"And you, daughter?"

Delia shook her head. "He makes the hairs on my arms rise straight up. No, Father. Lord Enaur would be a welcome addition, though."

Ucheni rang a small bell at the edge of his desk. A young page entered the room. "Get Lord Enaur, Captain Neoni, and Chief Scout Mysteso assembled for a meeting in the meeting room in an hour."

The boy nodded and sprinted off.

"Thank you, Master Kaepli. I'll see you in an hour."

The elf bowed and took his leave. Delia turned to follow when her father stopped her. "And what have you been doing today, Delia?"

I've been with Master Kaepli's apprentice, Sisruo, learning how to change my aura."

He leaned forward, elbows on the desk. "Show me."

Delia cleared her mind and began drawing power from her core. She struggled to get to her soul. It was difficult, almost painful to confront her raw being, but she tapped into that and thought black. Her father's gasp felt like a reward. She held the false aura for two minutes, the longest all day, before it slipped from her mind. Delia swayed with the effort and sank into the chair in front of his desk.

"That is incredible," he said. He poured water into a goblet and brought it around the desk to her. She drank it all and handed it back.

"Thank you. That's the longest I've held it."

He went back to his chair and dropped into it. "I wasn't

really convinced. I apologize. No one else can see Nethene's real aura, obviously, except you. How can that be?"

"He's a powerful elf, Father, and has had years of practice. Perhaps the aura everyone sees is the one he was born with and he just projects it while his real aura has changed to black. I have no idea."

Ucheni's fingers drummed on the arm of his chair. "Fair enough. Will you attend the council meeting?"

"If you need me to, Father."

"I do. You will be my left hand. Your mother," he said with a fond smile, "is already my right."

Delia smiled. "I accept, Father." She was truly happy to hear that. After so many years their welcome was unexpected but very real. The warm feeling of being loved and accepted wrapped around her and for the first time in her life, she actually felt safe.

His face dropped the smile. A look of sorrow took its place. "I am so sorry for sending you away. I shouldn't have done it."

She rose and went around the desk to him and kissed his cheek. Delia was still upset about being sent away but it was obvious both of her parents loved and missed her. Their auras didn't lie. "You made a terribly hard choice that you thought would protect me." She held out her arms and made a twirl. "Look. It worked. Think no more about it. I'm here now."

He rose and gave her a hug. "Thank you, Daughter." He held her by the shoulders and stood back, studying her. "Have you eaten?"

"Hours ago, it seems."

He rang his desk bell. Another page popped in the door. "Bring a plate of small sandwiches, any kind, water, and wine. Soon, please. I have a council meeting in an hour."

The boy ran off and the king and Delia sat in the

armchairs in front of the fireplace. "Let's talk until the food comes."

"That will be nice, Father."

"Tell me about the caravan," he asked.

Flashes of the bad things ran through her mind. She pushed them away. There were bright spots. She told him about those.

CHAPTER 14

Delia was in the practice yard. It felt good to move after spending hours in the mage's room and then in council with her father. There had been much gazing at maps as they tried to figure out what woods and what lake Mage Kaepli had seen. Decisions were finally made, and scouts would be sent out any minute now. Main troop forces would be sent when word came back from the scouts.

The practice field was nearly empty as most of the warriors practiced in the morning. Delia was moving through the katas for the staff, moving slowly to make sure she made each move correctly, then adding speed a bit at a time, always working to make the move perfectly. By the time she was satisfied, she was dripping with sweat and the sun was heading for the horizon.

The sound of clapping behind her gave her a start and she turned, staff at the ready. It was Sisruo.

"Well done, Princess!"

Pleased to see him, she felt a blush rising, but knew it was hidden by a face already flushed from exercise. "Thank you. Do you work with weapons?"

Sisruo walked over to her. "Alas, I do not." He patted his stomach. "I fear I do too much sitting and studying and not enough weapons work."

He looked perfectly slender and fit, very fit, to Delia. "I was about to practice with my fire balls. Would you care to watch?"

"I heard that you have mastered the art. I'd love to."

She put the staff back in the rack and motioned for him to walk with her. "I don't think I've mastered the art, yet, but I'm a fair marksman with them."

At the spot she practiced this skill, she stopped. "Stay behind me."

He gave her a small bow and stepped back.

Her first fire balls were a little sloppy. Mortified, she refocused. The next few were better and thrown about the furthest she'd ever done.

Sisruo clapped again. "How do you do it?"

As she did for the warriors, she walked him through what her process was. He was a quick learner. *Probably because he's already a mage, or near enough*, she thought.

They stood side by side and made a contest of who could throw fireballs the farthest, then which could form the biggest. She beat him, though, when she demonstrated making several at a time and throwing them one at a time.

He beamed at her. "I see I'll have to practice."

"Do mages go to war?"

He shrugged. "Sometimes. I think this time we will."

"We?"

"Master Kaepli and myself. Perhaps a few of the more advanced apprentices."

Delia felt a real fear for the old mage. She truly liked him. "Isn't Mage Kaepli a bit old?"

Sisruo laughed. "Don't let him hear you saying that." He

drew a deep breath. "He's as sharp a mind as I've ever met and has forgotten more magic than I will ever know. He will be a huge advantage for your father, the king, against your uncle."

Delia realized she was juggling fireballs as Sisruo spoke. She extinguished them immediately as a blush crept up her cheeks. "Sorry. It's become, um, natural, I guess, to make them."

"I wondered. You didn't seem to know you were doing it."

"Sometimes I don't." She thought back to the council meeting where she'd made one in response to her fear of Nethene. "I think I should prepare for dinner." They began walking back to the castle. "I don't remember seeing you there?"

"Oh no. I'm just an apprentice. That's not the place for me. Besides," he said quickly, "I'm usually studying one thing or another. We apprentices have a small dining room where we eat. That usually turns into another session on what we're working on."

"So you never stop working?"

"Oh, at mid-winter feast, we do. A lot of fun happens at mid-winter."

A stab of regret hit Delia hard. She didn't know any holidays of the elves. Her throat tightened with loss and regret.

Sisruo stopped and turned to her. "Oh. I'm sorry. I've hurt your feelings." His apology was instant and sincere.

Delia swallowed her grief and put on a smile. "Don't be concerned. I'll see for myself at mid-winter."

"Perhaps, sometime, you could come to the apprentice's dining room and eat with us. Everyone would be eager to hear about your study of aura changing."

For some reason, the invitation annoyed her. "Perhaps," she said a little harshly.

They had reached the doors into the castle. Sisruo stopped and bowed. "I must go this way, Princess, back to work, I'm afraid."

She bowed curtly. "So you must. Good evening." Delia turned and went past the guards who held the door for her, leaving Sisruo staring. All the way back to her room she fumed. Why had she become so annoyed with him? The more she thought about it, the more annoyed she became with herself.

In her room she peeled off her dress and boots and threw them on the floor. She stomped to the basin and pitcher and, after pouring water into the basin, held her hand over it, not quite touching, as she tried to get her feelings under control. In a moment the water was steaming. A moment more and it was boiling. She snapped her hand back when it began to boil over the sides of the basin and brought her mind back to what she was doing. Her heart pounding, she reached out to touch the water. She stopped just above the liquid, feeling the heat rise from it. Delia stepped back and covered her face, pressing on her eyes. She'd never done that before and hadn't heard that anyone could.

Anger gone, she poured more water into the basin to cool it and washed the sweat away. In a dressing gown, she brushed out her hair and thought about it. Why had she done it? Anger, she decided. *I was angry and it wasn't enough to throw my boots.* In the mirror, she could see the basin behind her. She got up and went to the bowl. The water was now room temperature. Delia held her hand over the water and thought about how she felt before. It took longer but the water began to steam.

Snatching her hand back she went back to her dressing table. After a deep breath, she began brushing her hair again. Another tool. *A weapon*, she thought. *I'll have to practice that in the yard tomorrow to see how it can be made effective.*

CHAPTER 15

I t was four days before the first scouts came back to the castle, then several arrived all in the same day. The king held a council meeting, again, not inviting Nethene.

"The scouts are all back," the king began. "We now know where the majority of my Uncle Iyuno's forces are or are headed." He stroked his chin. "It's going to be a fight. He has acquired a much larger force than ours. We'll have to fight smart and, perhaps, as my conversations with Captain Neoni have revealed, only one group at a time."

Lord Enaur spoke as everyone pondered that approach. "Won't they just regroup at the next location, Sire?"

"It's a possibility," Captain Neoni said. "But one we'll have to accept. We will have to defeat each force totally and then move to the next, quickly, and with luck, before Iyuno knows what happened to them."

"To the death, then?" Chief Scout Mysteso looked dismayed.

"I understand your concern, Mysteso." King Ucheni gave the scout a nod. "We don't usually kill our fellow elves and perhaps we may not have to this time." The king waved to Mage Kaepli.

"I may have a way to..." the old elf hesitated. "To suspend the fighters, for a time."

Mouths fell open around the table, Delia's included. That seemed impossible. "What happens when they wake?"

The others nodded curious to know the answer.

"We can wake them one at a time, then determine their reasons for joining Iyuno. He may have coerced them. In that case, war over, we can release them to their families. In other cases, they may have been lied to. Or perhaps the elf has a grievance that wasn't addressed properly. In all of those cases we have a chance to bring the elf and his or her family back into the fold. Those who are actually on Iyuno's side, well," the old elf sighed, "we'll have to take more drastic measures."

Delia thought she understood what that meant. Death to those elves.

"And how do you put an entire field of elves in suspension?" Lord Enaur had both hands on the table as he leaned forward.

"Not the whole field at once. A group at a time. I and three apprentices have the skill. It shouldn't take long."

Captain Neoni pulled at an ear lobe. "In the meantime, they'll be fighting. We could still lose many a fine elf."

"We could. We'll work as fast as we can." Mage Kaepli looked to the King. "It's your decision, Sire."

King Ucheni tapped his long fingers on the table. Delia saw the emerald ring on his left hand flash in the sunlight that spilled across the table. She wondered how he could bear to make such a decision. As his heir, she wondered how she would be able to make such a decision. Being a slave had not prepared her for that kind of burden.

"Very well," the king said. "We leave in three days. Prepare the troops. Send messages to the homesteads that we'll need every able-bodied elf. In the meantime, let's prepare a route from one force to the next that is both the most efficient and that will take us to my uncle with as little notice as possible. We don't want to waste energy riding back and forth across the realm for no reason."

The councilors stood, bowed, and left the room. Delia remained. She stood and put a hand on her father's shoulder. "A heavy decision, Father."

He nodded. "Very. I know many of the elves who have joined my Uncle. Kaepli was correct in his assessment of why some joined Iyuno. If they'd have just talked to me."

"Uncle must have poisoned their thoughts, Father. That can be the only reason."

"I hope so." The king rose. "The others, I'm sure, are already in the map room. As much as I'd like to join them, I'm going to let them hash it out for a time, then check on them." He gave her a smile. "What will you do?"

"I'm to the practice field. I'm experimenting with my powers. I may have something to show you before we leave."

His eyebrow rose. "Indeed. I'm eager to see it." They walked to the door. "Your mother and I are having a quiet dinner in our rooms this evening. Would you join us?"

"I'd love to." She gave him a peck on the cheek and said farewell. He headed to his office. She went to the practice grounds.

She set up archery dummies at the far end of the grounds, at various distances from where she'd stand. At her starting line, she focused. It had been a few days since she'd boiled the water in her basin. Since then, she'd figured out how to make the heat a focused blast. Not fireballs. The heat blasts were invisible. At this time, she could form the blast into a small radius and send it out twenty feet at full heat. Her goal was to get it to one hundred feet at full heat. For now, a blast was only air temperature when it reached the farthest goal.

The dummy at twenty feet flew backward, on fire. The one at thirty feet burst into flame as it rocked. The one at forty feet took a few moments of Delia holding the blast on it before it began to smoke. At fifty feet there didn't seem to be any reaction. Delia wiped the sweat from her forehead and took a sip from her canteen. Why couldn't she get farther than forty feet? Was that the limit of the power? What if she narrowed the width of the blast? She took another drink as she thought about how to do that.

"Delia?"

She turned. Her heart sped up and she smiled, all of her previous anger at him gone. "Sisruo. What brings you out here?"

He was eyeing the blazing archery targets. "Practicing your fireballs?"

"No." She shook her head. "A new power I'm developing —a heat blast. Its advantage is that it's invisible."

His eyebrows rose. "I didn't know such a power existed."

A wave of pride flowed through her. "Neither did I until a few days ago. I found it by accident."

CHAPTER 16

Sisruo turned back to her. "I'm here from Master Kaepli. He wondered if you would consider joining us in suspending the enemy fighters."

It was Delia's turn to be surprised. "He doesn't have enough mages to succeed?"

Sisruo's shuffling gave away his answer. "Not really. He spoke positively at the council meeting but he feels the more elves he has available to do the work, the better off we'll be."

"I'll be at my father's side."

"That's perfect. You could suspend anyone who closes in on the king."

Delia thought about it. She had it in mind to use her fire-balls and heat blasts to keep the enemy from her father. But as she thought about it, wasn't it better to hold the elves rather than kill them? "I'll do it. Will you teach me?"

"Yes, Princess. That's what the Master has suggested."

Delia nodded and cleared her mind from thinking about heat blasts. "Very well. What do I do?"

They spent until sunset practicing. "How do I know I'm doing it right?"

"Tomorrow, come to the Mage's study room. We'll practice on the apprentices who already know how."

Delia shook her head. "What if I make a mistake? I could kill someone!"

"That's how we all learned. And we'll teach you to unsuspend them, too."

Delia thought this a bad idea but couldn't think of any other way to test her skill. "What about practicing on an animal. A dog or a pig?"

"They aren't the same size. They would take a lot less power to suspend. It has to be a full-grown elf."

"Very well." She rubbed an eye. "Tomorrow after breakfast?"

Sisruo nodded. "After breakfast then." He looked at the sky. The first stars were already beginning to shine. "Shall I walk you to the castle?"

Delia swallowed her annoyance. He didn't think she was helpless. He was just being polite. "Thank you."

They walked in silence, Sisruo with his hands clasped behind him. "Master Kaepli is worried about you."

"Why?" Again, she had to work to be polite.

"You're new to your powers, Princess. That is all. Both I and Master Kaepli are surprised and amazed at how you've adapted to your new position. That change could not have been easy."

It wasn't easy, she thought better of saying. "It has had its challenges."

Sisruo chuckled. "Diplomacy must have been a birthright, Princess. You're a natural."

She had to smile at that. "Sometimes. I was hurt, you know. For years. I thought I was abandoned."

"I cannot fathom it, Princess. And I regret it with my whole being."

"Nothing to do with you, Sisruo. And Father and Mother have been so loving since I've returned. They apologize constantly."

The two arrived at the gate. The guards opened the door for her. ,

"In the morning, Princess." Sisruo bowed.

"In the morning, Sisruo."

The next day she went to the workshop where she'd first researched changing her aura. She still practiced that every day and was getting stronger and holding the aura longer. But this morning Mage Kaepli, Sisruo, and three other apprentices were waiting for her. She was introduced to Couran, Pelan, and Kaya. Kaya was the youngest and female. Her blond hair was plaited into many braids and pulled back into a pony tail which hung down her back to her hips. Couran and Pelan were cousins, brawny, as though they worked with weapons. "We do!" they chimed in unison when she asked. "Our uncle is Captain Neoni. He was disappointed when we chose to become mages but forgave us anyway." The two of them laughed.

Kaepli clapped his hands. "Let us begin. Kaya, you go first."

Delia watched as the young woman, not much older than herself, suspended Pelan. He sank slowly to the floor, eyes closed, seemingly asleep.

"Try to rouse him," Kaepli told Delia.

She walked over and crouched down. No amount of shaking or calling his name roused him. "He's truly suspended, Mage Kaepli."

"Kaya, wake him."

The young elf held her hands over him and chanted. Pelan woke slowly and sat up, rubbing his eyes. "Nice little nap."

The apprentices chuckled as Kaya gave him a hand to his feet. "Now you, Delia."

"I'll be your partner," Sisruo said as he stepped into the circle. He looked at her confidently and gave a small nod of support.

Delia wiped her hands on her skirt. She had felt confident yesterday evening but now, what if she killed him? Her hands trembled with fear.

"You can do it, Delia," Mage Kaepli said. "Just trust your instincts."

Her instincts were telling her this was a bad idea. But Sisruo gave her a smile and the others were speaking words of encouragement, so she held out her right hand and focused, just like last evening. Sisruo sank to the floor. For a moment she panicked, thinking she'd killed him. She was still staring at him, heart racing, when everyone began clapping. "Well done, Princess," Kaya said.

"Here's the waking spell," Mage Kaepli said. He said the spell three times. Delia held her hand over Sisruo and took a deep breath. She chanted the words, focusing on the elf on the floor. She could feel the power running from her to him. He didn't move. She looked in fright at Mage Kaepli. Already she was breathing fast, sure she'd killed him.

"Wait. It takes a moment."

It didn't seem to take so long when Kaya brought Pelan back, she thought. Then Sisruo moved. She let out a breath she hadn't realized she'd been holding.

He sat up. "Well done, Princess."

Everyone clapped again as Delia helped him to his feet.

"That was exciting." He dusted himself off and grinned.

"We'll practice a bit more today. Then every day until the army leaves." Mage Kaepli left the room.

Delia nodded. Another tool under her belt. It felt good.

CHAPTER 17

The day came for them to march off to the first location at which her grand-uncle had set up troops. Her horse constantly bobbed its head up and down and shifted left and right. Delia did her best to calm herself before trying to calm the horse because it was picking up her feelings. Finally, her father, the king, rode up. The Captain shouted out the order to proceed, and she followed the rest of the elves in the king's retinue out of the castle gates. A company of elves rode ahead of them while the rest of the force followed behind the king. Now that they were moving, she felt better. Sitting and waiting was difficult.

Sisruo rode up and moved into position beside her. He nodded toward Mage Kaepli who rode beside the king. "I was chosen to be his body servant."

"Quite the honor," Delia replied. She looked over him and his horse. He had dressed himself and his horse simply, as she had. There were no silver decorations on bridle or saddle. The sword at his side was plain, no fancy guard or decorations on the scabbard. A simple gray cloak hung from his shoulders over brown and green tunic, leggings and boots. Similar to her own dress, except for her hood. She had that on to hide her hair. She more than felt conspicuous, the one black head in a sea of blond.

"Yes. It is. I'm honored and hopeful I don't make a mess of it."

"Not likely. He seems to like you very much."

"True. But that has only made him harder on me." He gazed off into the distance over the heads of the king and the mage. "He's convinced me to take my final testing when we return."

"Good. It's time. You seem to have an excellent grasp of magic." She shrugged. "At least to my eye."

Sisruo chuckled. "Kaepli said pretty much the same. Said I was just dilly-dallying. 'Get on with it'."

Delia had to chuckle in return. "Very direct."

"Indeed."

They spoke often over the next four days as they marched to battle. The sound of tack jingling and rattling covered their conversation from others in formation. What Delia found annoying was the constant dust. It filled every crevice in skin and clothing and she was at the front. She couldn't imagine what the dust was like at the rear of the line.

When they camped for the night the fourth day, her father called a council.

"Have we found Nethene?" the king asked as they stood around a map of the area spread across a rough table.

Captain Neoni shook his head. "No. There's been no sign of him since four days before we left the castle. The men I had watching him had to be left behind with a guard when we rode. They still hadn't woken from whatever spell he used on them."

The king nodded and looked at Mage Kaepli. "And you?"

"I can see Iyuno's forces ahead. Nothing more than that."

Chief Scout Mysteso spoke up. "I sent scouts ahead; they've just returned. It looks like about a thousand elves, half on horseback, the rest on foot. There are humans, as well, Sire."

King Ucheni's eyebrow rose. "Humans?"

Mysteso nodded. "More than likely mercenaries, Sire. Swords for hire, is my guess."

The king rubbed his face, the beginning of a beard already growing. "That could mean that Iyuno isn't as well supported as we thought. Humans also means less magic and more fighting." He sighed. "And I'm sure Nethene has already joined my Uncle Iyuno." He blew out his breath. "There's nothing we can do about it now."

He pointed at the map. We break our force into three parts. I'll take the center, here." He tapped the map at a point mid-way along the valley floor. "Captain Neoni, take the right, Mysteso, take the left." Ucheni looked to the mage. "And you, Master Kaepli. I've heard you have a weapon."

"One I hope, Sire, will spare many elf lives. I and my apprentice Kaya, will be in Chief Scout Mysteso's force. My right-hand apprentice, Sisruo, and apprentice Couran will be with Captain Neoni. Apprentice Pelan will ride with you."

"Only one mage with me, Kaepli?"

"Oh no, Sire. Your daughter is well trained in the new method. She'll be by your side as planned." The old elf gave Delia a quick wink.

Her father turned to her. "Well done, daughter. You seem to be a formidable force all on your own."

A blush began to creep up her cheeks and she stared at the map. "I will do my best to protect you, Father."

He clapped her gently on the shoulder—a smile on his face. "I couldn't ask for a better daughter."

"Thank you, Father." She kept her eyes on the maps.

Praise from him, and trust, in front of all of these people. Delia held back tears; she didn't know whether they were tears of happiness or gratitude.

Ucheni drew a deep breath. "That's all for tonight. Get your rest. We'll need it."

Delia returned to her tent. She was still amazed that the baggage train had one just for her. She splashed her face and took off her boots, then lay down on her pallet fully clothed. The weather was still warm enough that she didn't bother with the finely woven wool blanket provided. She stared at the top of the tent, lit in waves by the torches around her father's tent. The light flickered and moved as the gentle breeze blew the flames

After the big build-up by Mage Kaepli, she hoped she could carry out her duties to protect her father. She pressed her fingertips against her eyes. Not a good horsewoman, she hurt from head to toe, especially after four days in the saddle. That didn't help her sleep. Even if she did drift off, random spasms in her legs jerked her back awake. To try and lull herself to sleep, she muttered the chant to awaken someone from suspension. A yawn in the middle of one iteration was so wide her jaw cracked. She worried about her father. What if he went charging ahead? Could she keep up? How long could she keep up the pace of suspending elves and throwing fireballs?

It was all a swirl in her mind until scratching at the tent door woke her. "It's daybreak, Princess. We have mush and tea ready at the fire."

Delia suppressed a groan. It hadn't felt like any sleep at all. "I'll be right there. Thank you."

The elf left and Delia rolled from her pallet. She stretched as best she could and pulled on her boots. It was going to be a long day.

CHAPTER 18

The King's force lined up on one end of the valley. Facing them, Iyuno's force filled the other end. She didn't see the humans, so they might be off to one side or another, as Mysteso's and Neoni's forces were, hidden in the woods. At her father's signal, a soldier blew his horn and the standard bearer dropped the flag, signaling the start of battle. The elves around her roared and kicked their horses forward. She remained in place, to the right of her father, who watched as his elves raced into the center of the valley.

Iyuno's forces did the same. Delia switched to her magical sight. There were no black auras. "Father, I don't see Nethene's aura in the other force."

Ucheni nodded. "He's probably with some other force. We'll find him eventually."

Her horse danced and Delia had to keep pulling it into line while she watched the opposing forces close on each other, the center of each line meeting in the middle with a crash and a roar. She could feel gooseflesh rise on her arms at the hue and cry that rose over the field in front of her.

Her father's forces held, and she could see opposing elves

dropping one by one from their saddles. Pelan must be in there somewhere, using the sleeping spell. Arrows rose and fell, elves screaming with pain as they were hit. A small party of five broke away and headed for the King. Delia kicked her horse forward and of its own volition, a fireball formed in her hand. As the five grew closer, she readied the ball, hurling it as far as she could. She didn't want them to get close to the king. The ball hit the lead rider, knocking him from his horse. The horse screamed and reared, kicking the horse next to it and causing confusion. In no time, all of the horses were screaming. The sound gave Delia chills. She threw another fireball at the horses. Again, rearing and screaming, the elves could barely control their mounts.

Still the elves grew closer. One elf in particular seemed able to control his horse while shouting instructions to the others. She chanted the sleeping spell and cast it at him. She saw him shake his head. He was too far away. She threw another fireball, hitting him in the chest. He dropped from his horse and rolled on the ground, putting out the fire. Too close! Too close! She tried the spell again. He rolled across the ground, the spell missed! He grabbed his horse and leapt into the saddle. She threw ball after ball at the now four elves. Two hit, and the elves fell. Two were left.

"Daughter, be careful!"

"Yes, father."

She tried the spell once more. One elf fell. One more to go, the calm one. She cast the spell; it hit him just fifteen feet away. The King kicked his horse to the left while Delia urged her mount right. The enemy horse raced through the middle and disappeared behind them. The elf lay asleep on the ground in front of them. Two of the King's elves dragged the enemy elf out of the way and remounted.

"Well done, daughter."

"Thank you, father."

Delia tried to still her shaking hands. That was too close. Perhaps she should have used her repeller power or the heat blast. She had to admit that she panicked. I'll do better next time, she thought to herself, then turned her attention back to the battle. There was so much dust it was hard to tell what was going on. King Ucheni kicked his horse to a walk and advanced. Delia wanted to tell him to stay back but bit her tongue. It was his place to be in the battle. It was her job to keep her eyes open and protect him.

The horn blew again, and Captain Neoni's forces came out of the woods just as a company of humans came out of hiding. They joined behind the first battle. The humans were on foot. Captain Neoni's force formed a circle around the humans. Delia saw them dropping. Sisruo and Couran were wielding the sleeping spell with good result. It didn't take long for all of the humans to be lying on the grass.

It was different with Captain Mysteso. The group he faced seemed to have their own spells. Elves burst into flame though Delia didn't see any fireballs. She had to stop looking there as her father had reached the first battle. She chanted the sleeping spell non-stop, elves dropping in front of her like cord wood. Twice she had to kick her horse out of the way of swinging blades. Her father drew his sword and entered the fray. It seemed forever to Delia before the opposing force's numbers were noticeably fewer. Her father wiped his blade and Delia took a breath. Was it over? She started to ask her father when something hit her in the back of the head. She could hear herself whimper and slump in the saddle. Then all went black.

CHAPTER 19

Delia woke in her tent with a headache that hurt even more when she opened her eyes. Her hand drifted to her head where she found a bandage. The back of her head was very tender and she winced as she gently probed the spot.

"Ah. You're awake!" Master Kaepli entered the tent. "I've brewed you some medicine for the pain."

Sisruo followed with a tray holding a pitcher and a horn mug. He put the tray on a small table and poured from the pitcher into the mug. "This should ease the headache."

Kaepli bent over Delia and looked into her eyes. "How do you feel?"

"Like I've been hit in the head."

He chuckled. "A sense of humor is a good sign." He checked the bandage.

"What happened?"

Sisruo handed her the mug. "Drink."

Delia did as he bid. The liquid tasted like dirt and mold. Her face scrunched up and she handed back the mug. "Can I have water?"

"Certainly." Kaepli nodded at Sisruo, who hurried off.

"So what happened?"

"An enemy was wounded and playing dead. When you stopped near him he took advantage of your back to him and threw a rock."

"He did a good job. What happened to him?"

"Your father's guard killed him."

Delia was surprised at a welling of sadness. She hadn't felt that way while the battle was raging. "That's a shame."

Kaepli nodded. "It is. And all for jealousy and envy. Brother against brother."

Sisruo returned with another pitcher. He poured some into the horn mug, rinsed it, tossed the water out of the door, then poured a mug full. He handed it to her. "Something a little more palatable."

Delia drank it all, enjoying the taste of the clean water. "Thank you. I was very thirsty."

"I told the King you're awake. He sends his regards."

"Thank you, Sisruo. He's all right?"

"Yes. The battle was over when you were hit. He's questioning prisoners or he'd come to see you."

"Are they telling us anything useful?"

"No. Well, yes," Kaepli said. He pulled the stool over to the bed and sat down. "As we suspected, most of the elves were misled. They joined Iyuno because of falsehoods. Many have re-sworn to your father." He stroked his beard. "They're telling us everything they know about his forces and locations. There are some that hate your father and are loyal to Iyuno. Those we will have to keep prisoner."

"What about the humans?"

"They're being woken one at a time. The first one we woke pointed out their leader. He confirmed that they were paid by Iyuno. The leader agreed to take his forces back to his own land. They're no longer a threat. They'll leave in the morning."

"Poor Father. He must be exhausted."

Kaepli chuckled. "He is determined. I'll make sure he rests and gets some food into him." The mage stood up. "And you must rest as well. Try to sleep through the headache. I'll leave the medicine here. If you still have a headache after we bring you supper, take another mug full."

"Thank you. I appreciate the help."

Sisruo held open the tent flap for the mage. "Sleep well, Princess."

"Thank you, Sisruo."

He stepped outside and dropped the flap. Delia sighed. Much had happened while she was unconscious but nothing that she could have helped with anyway. She turned onto her side so she wasn't lying on her wound and drifted off to sleep.

She was woken by her father's voice. "May I come in?"

Delia struggled to sit. "Yes. Of course."

The king entered, followed by an elf she didn't know carrying a tray with bowls. "I've brought you dinner. I thought I'd have my dinner with you."

The elf put the pitchers of water and medicine on his tray then placed his tray on the one on the table. He pulled the stool around for the King to sit.

"Thank you. We'll be fine here."

The elf bowed and left.

Ucheni handed her a bowl and a spoon. "Stew." He grinned. "Just like every other night."

Delia smiled back. "Indeed."

"How are you feeling?"

"Master Kaepli's medicine worked. The headache is much lessened. And I find that I'm hungry." She stirred the stew. Steam rose and brought her a savory scent. "Do I smell rosemary?"

"Yes. I heard one of the cooks found a patch and added some to the stew. It makes it a little different, at least."

Delia took a spoonful. It was tasty. "I was told you spent the afternoon questioning prisoners."

The king nodded as he chewed. "Yes. A weary afternoon as I heard the stories they related about Iyuno's lies." He stirred the stew in his bowl. "Unfortunate. More so those that joined Iyuno because they believe in him. I don't understand it at all."

Delia nodded. "A shame."

"It is." The king sighed and ate some more. When he swallowed, he said, "I'm sorry you were hurt."

A brief flash of memory of herself shaking after the close call with the attacking elf made her shudder but she did her best to conceal that from her father. She shrugged. "It was a battle, Father. No one should expect to come out unscathed."

"Still. I regret your injury."

"Master Kaepli has treated me well. I suspect I'll be up and about tomorrow." She stirred her stew around in the bowl. "When do we leave?"

"Soon. Perhaps tomorrow. We've learned all we can from the elves who've rejoined me. Later I'll meet with my council and we'll make a plan. I don't want to chase Iyuno's forces all over the countryside. If the information is correct, we'll go straight to my uncle and finish this."

"That would be good."

His face was grim. "We lost too many good elves today. On both sides."

Delia reached out and patted his hand. "It's not your fault, Father."

He sighed. "True. But it doesn't make me like it."

She nodded. They sat quietly after that and ate. He put the empty bowls on the tray when they finished. "Can I get you anything?"

"No, Father. I'm fine. I'll probably go back to sleep."

"Good. You rest." He kissed her on the head and left.

Not long after, the same elf came and picked up the tray. "Shall I get you more water, Princess?"

"No thank you. The pitcher has enough."

He bowed and left.

Delia settled into her cot and drifted off to sleep thinking about her father's grief.

CHAPTER 20

In the morning, after the mage had redressed her head, Delia went to the king's tent. "May I come in, Father?" she asked at the open tent door.

"Of course!" He beamed up at her from his table strewn with papers. "A welcome break."

Delia stepped inside. "Mage Kaepli told me you decided to wait here another day."

The king nodded. "It gives the wounded time to recover. You look well."

"The wound hurts and I still have a headache but not like yesterday. I'll be fine."

"Good. We will leave at first light tomorrow. Rest well."

Delia came around his table and kissed him on the head. "Thank you." She went back to the door. "I think I'll stroll around a little and work the stiffness out of my legs. Then rest awhile."

"Good idea. Take care."

"I will, Father." Delia left the tent and looked around the camp. Everything spiraled out from the king's tent. She began to stroll, enjoying the sunshine and fresh air. The tent was fine but as the day got warmer, it began to smell musty. She was glad to be outside. At the mage's tent, she found all of the apprentices gathered. "Hello."

"Hello! We're glad to see you up," Kaya said. "Sisruo told us you were feeling better." Kaya grinned at him as he blushed.

Delia saw the blush and could feel the heat rise on her cheeks as well. "Master Kaepli was most helpful."

"Do you still have a headache?" Sisruo asked.

"A little, but nothing I can't handle."

Sisruo leapt to his feet. "I'll make more of the headache potion."

"No, thank you. I'm fine. What about the other wounded?"

"They're over in the hospital tents. Most will be able to ride tomorrow. The rest will stay here with the guards surrounding the prisoners." Couran rose from his squat as he finished speaking. "We're taking a quick break from the morning's healings. Then we'll bring them all food and more water."

Delia nodded. "I'm just working the kinks out, then I'll be back to my tent."

"You're going to keep walking?" Sisruo's tone of voice indicated his alarm.

"Is there some reason I shouldn't?" Delia saw Pelan swat Sisruo in the calf from where he was sitting on the ground. Pelan had a grin across his face.

"Well. I, uh, no, I suppose not." He blushed again as Kaya snickered. "I'll walk with you."

Delia arched an eyebrow. "Thank you. That would be nice." So, from the others' reactions, he likes me as much as I like him, she thought. A tiny smile crept to her face.

As Sisruo hurried to her side, Couran and Pelan both laughed. Delia hid the smile. "Let's go then."

They strolled past the Captain's tent and then Mysteso's. She realized she could tell whose rank and status was higher by the tent arrangements. As they walked, she made note of the walking wounded. They nodded to her as she passed and nodded back. "So many hurt!"

Sisruo grimaced. "Using the healing arts, we put many back on their feet. Some, though, were hurt too badly for the healing to do much except take away some of the pain or fix minor problems. Kaya has volunteered to stay behind when the camp breaks to look after the ones not able to travel."

"That was nice of her."

"Her healing gift is better than the rest of ours. It's a good choice."

Soon they came to the hospital tent and Delia went inside. She spoke briefly to each elf, holding their hand or laying her hand on a fevered forehead. "They're so nice to me," she said after they left.

"They saw you are wounded. They feel as though they share a bond with you now."

"Perhaps so." Delia was lost in thought about how well she was fitting in, given her upbringing, when a psychic blast knocked her sideways. "What?"

"Who did that?" Sisruo gave Delia a quick look over. "Are you all right?"

Delia shakily exhaled. "Yes. I think so."

Sisruo strode to the wooden fence holding the prisoner elves inside. "Who attacked her?"

The elves inside laughed and moved away from the fence.

Delia studied their auras. All of them were dark. One in particular though, drew her to the fence. She looked directly at the elf. "You know me?"

The elf made a mocking bow, a smirk on his face. "Who wouldn't know the poor princess Delia, robbed of her background. Forced to live with humans." The six other prisoners all laughed.

Delia could feel the scorn. She swallowed the insults. "You have me at a disadvantage. What's your name?"

By now the guards were surrounding the fence, spears ready.

"Ceinno." He made a sweeping bow.

Delia studied him. His aura was dark purple, almost black, like a fresh bruise. She wondered if that aura hurt. "You are a relative?"

"Not of a sniveling, human-raised abomination. I'm nephew to Iyuno."

"Then you share blood with my father and myself. Why this war?"

"My uncle is the better elf. He was cheated of his throne."

"Were you there?"

"No. But Uncle told me."

It was obvious to Delia, as she watched Ceinno's aura bubble and flash, that she wasn't going to change his mind. A brief thought about how her father's conversation went passed quickly and she left it alone. "I'm sorry this has happened. We're family."

Ceinno spat on the ground. "No kin of mine."

The evil permeated the stockade, rising from all seven elves. She turned to go. Sisruo took her arm. "Best to leave, Princess."

"Do you feel it?"

"Feel what?"

"The evil. It's thick over the stockade. I'm going to suggest to father that those seven be separated."

"Probably a good idea, Princess." Sisruo cut straight

through the spiral camp to the king's tent. He called out to the guard in front. "Her Royal Highness, Princess Delia, to see His Majesty, the King."

Delia had a moment of annoyance about him speaking for her but pushed it away. This was more important.

"Come in."

The King rose. "Are you all right, daughter?"

"Yes, Father. I am. I just came from the prisoner's stockade."

The king's face clouded. "I wish you hadn't."

"I met Ceinno. He is almost as evil as Nethene. I advise separating those elves. The entire stockade stinks of evil."

"What happened?"

"We were walking by. I wasn't even aware of the stockade. That's when a psychic blow nearly knocked me off of my feet."

The king glared at Sisruo. "You were with her?"

"Yes, Your Majesty. The prisoners were most disrespectful."

She wanted to defend Sisruo and was about to speak when Ucheni looked back to her. "I'll talk to Captain Neoni about it. You think they're dangerous?"

"Yes, I do."

The king sighed. "Very well. But stay away from there."

"Yes, Father."

She bowed and left, Sisruo behind her.

"Are you sure you're alright? That seemed like quite the blow."

"I'm fine. Just a little tired." She stopped at her tent. "I'll take a nap, I think."

"Good. If you need more headache medicine, let me know."

"Thank you, Sisruo." Delia went into her tent. It was warmer inside than out. All the better to sleep, she thought.

She lay down on top of the wool blanket and closed her eyes. Later, she woke once, drenched in sweat, a tiny scream escaping her. Delia reached for the mug of water and drank the whole thing. Shaking, the memory of the dream filled her thoughts. She was back at the caravan, in chains this time, a slave.

CHAPTER 21

Delia was awakened by a call at the door of her tent. "Princess, breakfast is being served."

Groggy, she responded. "Is it morning?"

"Yes, Princess. We leave as soon as we've eaten."

Delia blinked, her eyes gummy from sleep. "I'll be right there." She heard footsteps leaving as she swung her legs around to the ground. Morning already? She was still in her clothes. At the wash stand she splashed her face and rinsed her eyes. What had happened? Was she that tired? The nightmare niggled at the back of her mind. After unbraiding her hair and combing it, she rebraided it and stuffed her personal possessions into her saddlebag. Ready, she left the tent and went to the cook tent. There, people milled around, bowls of mush in hand, chatting. She thanked the elf who handed her a bowl and walked to a tree to sit, her back against the trunk.

Sisruo found her there, eating the last of her food. "Princess. I didn't see you at dinner last night." He sat down beside her.

"No." Delia thought about telling him about her dream. "I slept straight through."

"Is your wound bothering you?"

"No. I rebandaged it this morning after I combed my hair. It's fine." She saw him raise an eyebrow. "Just tired, I guess."

"Ceinno dealt you a huge blow yesterday. Could that be it?"

Delia shrugged. "I don't know. I don't feel any different." To herself, though, she wondered if Sisruo was right. Was the dream of her losing everything and returning to slavery part of the attack? "No matter. We leave today." She got up and dusted off her clothes. "I'll see you at the lineup."

Sisruo nodded but she could tell he wasn't happy with her explanation. After returning the bowl to the dish washers, she went to the picket line to get her horse ready. An hour later, she was in line with Sisruo and the Mage when the king rode up and the party marched off.

The march lasted three days. In that time she spoke with the Mage about the psychic blow she'd received and her unease at the after-effects. "It depends on many things," Kaepli said. "For example, you were already wounded, so that may be all it is." He studied her. "Your aura looks normal and you don't seem to be suffering any other effects except for the fatigue and night-mares. Those could be a result of the original injury."

"Thank you, Master Kaepli. I just wondered."

"Those kinds of attacks can be fatal. I'm glad you asked."

Delia nodded. "I didn't want to bother you."

He gave her a smile. "Never a bother to speak with you, Princess. Dreams are powerful things. And," he shrugged, "it's natural that you would fear going back to slavery. But I assure you, you are safe and loved here, despite Cienno's attack yesterday."

She nodded. That was enough for now, but it lingered in the back of her mind that she had a weakness that could cloud her judgement in certain circumstances. She'd have to watch out for that.

Soon, they arrived at a castle. It had a dark appearance, and to Delia, it felt evil. The moat around it was full and stakes had been placed in multiple rows all around the perimeter. Logs had been piled on all of the roads approaching the castle. Turning to her magical sight, Delia could see an aura hanging over the entire place. It was as black as Nethene's.

"I don't have a good feeling about this, Father," she said as she sat beside him. Their horses didn't seem to like the place either. They tossed their heads, snorting and danced around the dusty road.

"I don't much like it either. But if that aura is any indication, Iyuno and his minions, Nethene included, are all in there. I'll send a messenger."

Master Kaepli shook his head. "I'm afraid you'll lose any messenger, Sire."

Captain Neoni and Mysteso rode up. "A bad business, Sire," Neoni began. "I expected to see his forces outside the castle. See his forces, or at least watchers, as we neared."

Mystesto nodded his agreement. "They're up to something, Sire."

The king nodded. "Set up camp out of sight of the castle. We'll meet this evening. In the meantime, post watchers around the castle in pairs, for safety."

"As you will, Sire." With that, Neoni and Mysteso rode off.

The mage stroked his beard. "I'll use the scrying bowl. It may provide information."

"Very good."

The mage rode off. Sisruo rode with him.

Delia stayed with her father and his guards. "Do you have a plan, Father?"

"No." Ucheni shook his head. "No plan at all. Perhaps the mage will see something useful."

Delia hoped so as well.

She was present at the council meeting that evening. They stood around the rough table; a map of the area with Iyuno's castle in the middle, covered it.

The king asked, "Do we know what the inside of the castle looks like?"

Neoni shook his head. "We didn't even know a castle was here, Sire. He must have had it built recently."

Mage Kaepli entered the tent. "Your Majesty. I apologize for being late."

"You have information?"

The king looks tired, Delia thought to herself. *And no wonder. The fate of the entire kingdom rests on his shoulders.*

"Not as much as I would like." The mage spread a new map over the table. "This is the interior of the castle as best as I could see in the scrying bowl. The aura covers most everything in darkness."

The group huddled over the map. "There are a lot of blank spots," the king said.

"Yes, Sire. The blackness was too thick there for me to see."

Mysteso traced possible paths through the castle with his forefinger. "Some evil lurks in the blank spots, I'm sure."

Everyone agreed. The king sat down on a stool. "What about the blocked roads and the stakes? Can we get rid of them?"

"I have my apprentices working on that now, Sire." Kaepli pulled his sleeves into place. All of the materials are organic, so we may be able to pull them out of the ground to free our approach."

The king nodded. "Mysteso, what do your scouts say?"

"They see no one outside the castle, Sire. Whatever the inside is like, outside appears quiet."

There was a commotion at the door. It was Kaya, looking to Delia as though she hadn't slept in days.

"Your Majesty." She turned to the king. "The prisoners escaped. They killed all of the guards."

A gasp escaped from each elf in the meeting. "The wounded?" the king asked.

"They're fine. I left the most healthy in charge and rode here as directly as I could."

Delia thought the young apprentice looked about to drop from exhaustion.

"Thank you," the king said. He looked to Neoni. "Double the watchers. I don't want them to sneak into the castle."

Neoni bowed and hurried from the tent. "Master Kaepli, please take care of your apprentice. Let me know if you need anything." Kaepli bowed and he helped Kaya from the tent.

The king looked at Delia. "Separating them didn't seem to work. They have great power. Power I don't want added to Iyuno's."

"What do you need me to do, Sire?"

"Check for auras. See if you can identify anyone in the castle. Or around the castle, for that matter. Keep me apprised."

"Yes, Sire." She bowed and left the tent.

Outside she found Sisruo, pacing back and forth. "Hello!"

"Hello. You didn't come into the tent."

"No, Master Kaepli had work for me. Is the meeting over?"

"For me. I'm going to look at the castle and see if I can identify individual auras."

Sisruo gaped. "At night? From this distance?"

"From where I can. And yes, now."

"I'll come with you."

"Doesn't the Mage have work for you to do?"

"Not at the moment." He reached out to take her arm.

Delia pulled it out of his reach. She could only think of Emil, or the caravanners grabbing at her. "I'm capable of doing this on my own." Her voice was cutting.

Even by the light of the torches, she could see him blush. "I know you are. But we're outside of a deadly enemy's fortress."

Delia drew a deep breath. He had a point, and he wasn't a caravanner. Still, she had to keep in mind her fears and not react to every little thing so violently. "Very well."

CHAPTER 22

The enemy castle was over a mile away so Delia and Sisruo saddled their horses and rode out to a hillside overlooking the small valley where the castle stood.

Delia dismounted and tied her horse to a branch. Sisruo did the same. They stood just inside the tree line where, Delia hoped, they couldn't be seen.

"How do you propose to see inside the castle?"

"I don't know. Since Father asked it of me, I assumed it could be done." She could hear Sisruo draw a deep breath.

"I've never heard of it, but that doesn't mean it isn't possible. He may be relying on your magical strength."

Delia thought so too. She switched to her magical sight. "I don't see anyone's aura outside of the castle except our own watchers. What do you see?"

"Not much. Not at this distance."

She heard the disappointment color his statement. Another thing that made her different. "What I see is…I don't know what to call it, an aura of magic around the gate and the windows."

"They've set protection spells. It makes sense. Can you tell me what they look like?"

"They're lines of yellow, like hoops, around each opening. Over the entire castle is an aura of dark purple. At the windows, I can see some people, auras are all dark. I can't see through the walls. I've failed Father." Her shoulders slumped.

"I think not. You can see all of that when I can only see vague shimmers at best. I can't even see our watchers. The news about the protection spells is important. It will change how the king approaches the castle."

"I suppose you're correct." His comment did make her feel a little better. "We should get back and tell the council."

Once back, she spoke to the king and his councilors, telling them what she found. She did her best to make it all seem positive.

"Could you see the protection spells, Sisruo?" the mage asked.

"No, Master. I couldn't. Nor could I see our watchers. Not at that distance."

King Ucheni scratched at his beard. "What can we do about the protection spells?"

The mage spoke, "I'll have to think, Sire. I'd like to work with Delia to try and identify what's there."

The king looked over at her. "Are you ready for that?"

She nodded. "I am. Whenever you're ready, Mage Kaepli."

"Let's go to my tent. I'll look in my books." He gave the king a bow and headed for the door.

Delia and Sisruo did the same and followed the mage out. In Kaepli's tent, they all took stools around the table. Kaepli handed Delia parchment and pen. "Draw what you saw. The patterns may help me research."

While Delia drew, Kaepli pulled an ancient tome from a

chest in the corner of the tent. He brought it to the table and sat down. "Protection spells can be tricky. A simple one could prevent anyone or thing from entering or leaving. As you add requirements, say, allowing exit, or specifying various creatures or beings, the spell can become a threat to the setter as well as anyone trying to break it." He stroked his beard as he turned crackling pages.

Delia handed him the parchment. "I'm not a very good artist."

Kaepli took the page. "You described them as hoops. Were the yellow lines thick or thin?"

"They varied, and as you can see, the distance between them varied as well. These aren't identical representations. Just generalizations."

Kaepli sighed and put the drawing down. "That's all right. They may change constantly. But what you saw may help me pin down the spell." He continued to turn pages.

Sisuro rose and got them all mugs of water and put them on the table. "Unless you'd prefer wine, Master?"

"No, water is fine. Thank you."

Delia nodded her thanks and drank. She was getting a headache and wanted nothing more than to go to her own tent and sleep. Being a princess was tiring work. "What can I do to help?"

"Nothing, really, other than what you've done already." The mage continued to turn pages. "I may know what they're using but I want to be sure." He looked up at her, then raised an eyebrow. "Go. Rest. When I confirm my thoughts, we made need you to help us break the spell."

Delia nodded. "Very well." She stood up. "I'll leave you to it then."

She left the tent and walked the short distance to her own. Delia didn't bother to light the candle on her table but took off her boots and lay down on her cot, fully clothed. She wasn't looking forward to being the spell breaker. She didn't have the confidence in her own magic that everyone else seemed to have. It was still too new to her. Would they go to battle tomorrow? Iyuno must know that they were there. If she could see the watcher's auras, couldn't he? Or Nethene? She sighed and rolled over onto her side and tried to still the thoughts whirling around in her brain. Whether they went to battle tomorrow or not, she suspected it would be a full day for her. She needed her sleep.

She was woken in the dark by a sound of knocking on the tent pole. "Princess, Princess. Wake up! The king calls for you."

Delia rolled from the cot, bleary-eyed and confused. It was still dark. "What time is it?"

"Just before dawn. Please hurry?"

"Is the king all right?" She sat on the edge of her cot and began pulling on her boots.

"Yes. But hurry."

She couldn't think why the king would be calling her in such a hurry unless there was something very wrong. Was this someone trying to lure her away? "I'll be right there."

When she came out of the tent, the elf was still there. She'd seen him before. "This way Princess."

The elf hurried away, but not in the direction of the king's tent. With a sigh of relief at recognizing the servant, she scurried after the elf. Then a feeling of foreboding washing through her. What could be wrong?

CHAPTER 23

Delia shivered in the cool, pre-dawn air. It was wet, too, dew soaking her boots as they quickly walked to meet the king. "What's going on?"

"I am not the one to tell you, Princess." The elf hurried on and Delia, fuming, could do nothing but follow.

They soon arrived at the edge of the camp where elves stood with torches, and the king, with Kaepli and Sisruo next to him, stood in the center of the horseshoe shaped crowd.

"Sire. You called for me?"

"Yes. Thank you. Mage Kaepli believes he's found the correct protection spell." He nodded to the mage. "Begin."

The mage held out his hands. "I'm setting the spell around that boulder."

Delia switched to her magical sight. As the mage concentrated, she could see yellow lines of power around his hands. As they grew brighter, she could see them flow away and surround the rock. "There," he said as he dropped his hands, "it's one of the more powerful spells and modified, at that." He turned to Delia. "It was your description that helped me find the right spell. I am surprised that Iyuno or perhaps Nethene dared to modify that spell."

"And can you break it?" the king asked.

"Now that I know the spell, yes." The mage turned back to the boulder and raised his hands again.

Delia could see green lines of magic build, then flow to the rock, covering the yellow lines. The two merged and with a flash, disappeared. A sigh of surprise arose from the crowd.

"Well done, Mage Kaepli. Can you break the spells on the whole castle at once?"

"No Sire. Unfortunately, not. We'll need elves at each entrance to work the spells. I could use Delia's help."

The king turned to her and glanced at the bandage on her head. "Are you up to it, daughter?"

"I am well enough, Sire, to help the mage and his apprentices."

"It's settled, then. We will approach the castle at mid-morning."

With that the king left and the group dispersed except for the mage, Sisruo, and Delia. "How do I work the spell, Mage Kaepli?" Delia asked.

"I'll teach both you and Sisruo at the same time." He demonstrated again, this time telling them what he was doing. After two run-throughs, he had them practice. Delia thought it was much like casting an aura and after a try or two, managed to get the protection around the boulder. Sisruo took longer but he, too, eventually cast the magical protection around the rock. "That was hard." He wiped the sweat from his brow.

The mage looked about. "The sun is up. We'd better get back and eat, then prepare for battle."

Delia nodded and the three returned to the camp.

When the cohorts formed up, the mage was with Captain Neoni and Sisruo was with Mysteso. Kaya rode with Delia and the king. The other apprentices were split between Sisruo and Kaepli. "Mage Kaepli taught you the spell?" Delia asked Kaya.

"All of us." She edged her horse next to Delia's. "I have to say it took me awhile to get the hang of it."

"I just hope we can destroy the protection spells quickly." Delia coughed in the dust being raised by the fidgeting horses. "And that after, we can destroy the road barriers and the spikes."

"The rest of the elves can handle those," Kaya said. "We're the only ones who can take down the protection spells."

Delia felt better. Using magic took energy and she thought she'd need all she had to open the castle doors. Nagging at her was how Iyuno and Nethene would defend the place, especially if all of his forces were inside. She was no expert, but that didn't seem possible. "What other traps do you think they have?" she asked Kaya.

The elf turned to her. "Other traps?" Kaya shook her head. "None?"

A frown filled Delia's face. "I need to talk to the king." She applied heel to her horse and moved out of line, cantering up to her father. She edged up to his horse.

"Delia?" The king looked behind, then back at her. "Is everything all right?"

"I'm not sure, Father."

"What do you mean?"

"We've seen no elves outside Iyuno's castle. They have the roads blocked and spikes placed around the castle but no other defenses. I have to wonder how they plan on defending the place? Are there other traps we haven't noticed?"

Ucheni pressed his lips together and his forehead

furrowed. They trotted along like that for some time. He called the Sergeant of the Guards to him

The elf dropped back to ride on the right of the king. "Sire?"

"Send messengers to Neoni and Mystesto. Tell them to be on the lookout for other traps. Tell the Mage in particular that we suspect we've missed something. You be on the lookout along our path as well. This whole thing seems too easy."

The Sergeant nodded and prodded his horse forward, calling for messengers.

Delia sighed. "I'm sorry, Father. I feel as though I'm causing trouble."

He shook his head. "I should have seen it sooner. Thank you. You are quite right. This is too easy. Some logs and spikes and a well-seen door protection? Too little by far." He sighed. "Now I wonder if anyone is in the castle at all, let alone Iyuno."

"I saw auras through the windows, Father."

"True. But maybe only a few elves inside, and Iyuno and Nethene and Ceinno and the rest are somewhere else." He pounded a fist on his thigh. "I was too eager to end this."

They rode together in silence, just the jingle of harness and the dust of travel surrounding them. The advance guard easily removed the logs and when they got to them, the spikes. No other trap seemed to exist except the door protections. For that Delia and Kaya rode to the front.

Time to get to work.

CHAPTER 24

Delia walked up to the edge of the moat as Kaya stood a little to her right and behind her to back her up if necessary. Delia wiped her hands on her trousers then focused as she raised her hands. Her mouth was so dry her tongue stuck to the roof of her mouth. She refocused on the yellow bands, her energy forming the green magic. At the point when she thought she couldn't hold the magic any longer, she released it, watching it flow across the moat and cover the yellow bands. She kept feeding the magic, urging it to cover every yellow line, smother it, eliminate it.

Beside her, Kaya had her hands raised as well, green power circling her hands, ready to assist if needed. "You can do it," she whispered.

Delia gave a brief nod. She had to stay focused. It wasn't long before every yellow line was covered, but something was wrong. "It doesn't feel right."

"What do you mean?" Kaya looked at her, eyebrows high.

"It's not the same magic we practiced on. It's wrong."

"What's it doing?"

"Resisting, pushing back." Her arms began to shake with the effort. "I'm not sure I can hold it."

Kaya threw her magic at the bands. Delia could feel the other elf's strength and it helped but it wasn't going to be enough. "We have to build a wall. This is going to blow back on us and the army."

Kaya had beads of sweat running down her temples. "How did you hold this alone?"

"No idea." She drew a shaky breath. "Can you hold a few moments while I build a protection shield?"

Delia could see Kaya's entire body vibrate with her effort.

"A very short time."

"Here I go." Delia removed her green magic and, using the edge of the moat in front of her as an anchor, began to weave yellow bands in a circle. Around and around she went. Behind her she could hear her father ordering the army back. That was a little relief. She continued to build—around and around—until the yellow wall was two stories high. She whispered the command and dropped her arms. "Stop, Kaya!"

Kaya fell to the ground, panting, just as the protection on the gate flashed. Delia was knocked backward off of her feet, a wave of energy passing by, ruffling the grass and shaking nearby bushes. The army behind her roared. She twisted around to see what was happening.

Out of holes in the ground, elves swarmed, dressed all in black. She could see that most of them had auras dark as night. Shaking, Delia realized that she and Kaya were on the wrong side of that mass of elves.

She crawled over to Kaya, who was lying limp on the ground. "We must move!"

"What?" The maiden elf murmured weakly.

"The black elves are attacking from hidden tunnels. We're on the wrong side. Move!"

Delia helped Kaya to her feet and the two began working their way to the left at the edge of the moat. They hunched over, hoping to avoid being seen. Delia desperately wished for some bushes for cover but of course, none would be found this close to the moat. "We have to get far enough around the castle to cut back to the forest."

"Yes." Kaya was breathing harshly.

Delia didn't like the sound of it, but there was nothing she could do about it at the moment. Ahead, she could see the dust rising from Mysteso's force. "Look. The same thing happened to them."

Kaya raised her head. "Not good."

"Not at all. We'll try and cut into the forest here."

Kaya nodded and did her best to move quickly.

Delia tried to see all around her. Nothing was coming up behind them. Nothing was coming from Mysteso's direction either. They were closing in on the tree line. She began to think they were going to make it.

They ran into the shade, a blessing in itself. Kaya struggled to stay on her feet. "I have to rest."

Delia found a tree and helped Kaya sit, back against the trunk, on the side away from the fighting. She glanced around. They were alone. She knelt next to the apprentice. "Can you tell me what hurts?"

"Everything. I used the last of my strength to hold that spell." Kaya stopped, breathing hard. "Then when the spell snapped, even with your shield, it felt as though I'd been whipped."

Delia took a look at Kaya's aura. It was very faded. "I'm sorry. You've been injured in a way I don't know how to fix."

"I just need rest. It'll come back."

Delia sat back on her heels. They were in a fix. She couldn't carry Kaya. Two forces were fighting on either side of them. Neither of them had more than simple eating knives on them and they were cut off from their own side. Delia pressed her fingers to her temples as though that would generate an idea. All she could feel was panic.

"Take a breath."

Delia shook her head with confusion. "What?"

"Take a deep breath," Kaya said weakly. "I can see you're panicking. Just take a breath."

Delia felt like a selfish child that the injured elf had to comfort her. "Sorry. I don't know what to do." All she could think about was being taken and turned back into a slave. She took several deep breaths to clear her mind.

"That's fine. We'll get out of this."

Delia nodded. She refrained from asking how. She held Kaya's hand. "Of course, we will." As they sat, she listened to the battles on either side of them. The clang of sword on shield or sword on sword was loud. There was screaming, too, though she tried not to dwell on that. She worried about her father and the ambush. Was he safe? What about Mage Kaepli and Sisruo? Delia fought back the tears of fear and grief. *Stop being a baby. You can't stay here. Move!* "We need to move, Kaya. We're too close to the castle and the battle."

"Let's go then."

Delia helped her to her feet and they did their best to move quietly through the forest. "It's just a mile to our camp," Delia whispered. "Do you think you can go that far?"

Kaya nodded.

They edged around a large bush and when they were just beyond it, Delia heard a snap behind them. She turned around. Out of the bush emerged four male elves, dressed all in black like the ambushers. *There must be a tunnel in that bush,* she thought, just before one of the elves raised his hand and threw a blue ball of magic at them. She didn't have time to untangle herself from Kaya. She raised her free hand to try to repel the elf. It was too late. The ball hit them. Her last thought was, *No!*

CHAPTER 25

Delia woke in a stone room. Kaya was awake, huddled beside her.

"I've already walked the room. The door is solid oak with iron laced through it and locked. The window is too high for me to reach. Both of them have protection wards on them."

Delia touched the back of her head. Her fall, or perhaps the elves when they brought her here, knocked her wound open. It hurt and, she looked at her hand, it was bleeding. "Can you look at my head please? It's bleeding." She scooted around so her back was to Kaya. She felt fingers gently probe her head and part her hair.

"Oh, yes. It's broken open. Let me see if I can help."

Delia felt that spot on her head get warm and the pain went away. "That feels better."

"Good." Kaya sat back against the wall. "I was out long enough for my power to regenerate."

"I'm glad. Any idea how long we were unconscious?"

Kaya shook her head. "I'm not sure. I was totally drained when we were captured and I'm not sure how long it should or would have taken to get back to full strength. So, it could still be today or we may have lost a day. Or more."

"More?" Delia sagged against the wall. She thought about the battle that had been raging when they were captured. Was her father all right? What happened at the battle? Was he worried? Was he dead? A soft sigh escaped her lips.

"I know." Kaya took Delia's hand. "We don't know anything and it's easy to drop into despair. So let's tally up the good points. First, we're alive."

Delia chuckled. "I suppose that is a good point. Yes."

"Next, we seem to have all of our powers and faculties. Every body part works."

"That's so." Delia began to feel better. "And now that I think of it, my head was bleeding, and I'm not covered in blood so not too much time must have passed."

Kaya grinned. "That's true. Clever of you to think of that. I guess I was wallowing in some despair myself."

Delia patted Kaya's hand and let out a big breath. "The battle could still be going on." She stood up and looked up at the window. "You're smaller than I am. If you stood on my shoulders, do you think you could see outside?"

Kaya got up and stood beside Delia, looking at the window. "Maybe. Let's try it."

Delia went to the wall under the window and put her hands on the wall. "I'll make a knee so you can climb up."

Kaya took her boots off and placed her left foot on Delia's left knee. "I hope I don't hurt you too much."

"It'll be worth it if we can learn something." As Kaya shifted her weight to her right foot on Delia's right shoulder, Delia straightened up. "Are you close?"

"I'm still below the window. I'm going to try and pull myself up."

Delia felt the weight leave her shoulders, so she stepped back from the wall to see. Kaya had both hands on the window's edge, elbows bent as she made the effort to lift herself up. "Let me try to help." She dashed over to Kaya and put a hand under each of her feet. "I'm going to push up, Kaya." As she pushed, she focused and added a little power.

"It's working! Keep going!"

Delia lifted until her arms were straight up. "That's it. Can you see out?"

"A little. Tree tops mostly. Wait, listen." Kaya was silent for a moment. "I can hear fighting!"

"My arms are getting tired."

"Oh. Yes. You can let me down."

Slowly, Delia lowered her arms until Kaya's feet touched her shoulders. She braced against the wall again as the elf clambered down.

Kaya let out a big breath. "That was awkward."

Delia brushed off her hands. "What did you see?"

"The moat below us. Cleared ground on the other side of the moat to the tree line. That's it."

"How high up are we?"

"High. Four stories or more."

Delia paced off the dimensions of the room. Six paces to the door. Seven from one side of the room to the other. The room was clean, at least there was that. But it had no water or food and no place to relieve themselves, not even an empty bucket.

"The window is open?"

"Yes. Except for the protection spell. I could feel my fingers tingling on the window's edge."

"So we are stuck here until someone comes to let us out." Delia didn't like that at all. It felt like it had when she was a slave.

"Pretty much."

Kaya sat down, her back against the wall facing the door. "I'm going to take a nap."

Delia nodded. *Kaya must still be feeling the effects of her all out magical efforts from the morning.* But Delia wasn't tired. She paced back and forth in front of the door, stopping now and then to examine the door or parts of the wall. The sun set and the room grew dark and chilly. She finally went over to sit with Kaya. Delia found Kaya's body warmth comforting, even if it was just arm to arm. At least she wasn't alone.

When Kaya woke, the two traded stories about growing up. Delia found herself a little envious of Kaya's tales of family outings, trips to other elf kingdoms, and her siblings' antics, but the tales helped to pass the time and she was glad of that.

They were startled by the sound of a key in the lock of the door. It swung open on creaky hinges and they shielded their eyes at the glare of a torch. It was one of the black elves. "Come."

Delia scrambled to her feet. Kaya shoved her feet into her boots and rose also. "Where?"

The elf backed out of the room. "Come."

Delia sighed. There was nothing else to do. She followed the elf into the hall where she saw three others waiting. Kaya followed her.

"Come," the elf with the torch said once more. He led them down the hall to the left. Delia and Kaya walked side by side, the three other black elves following. They reached the end of the hall in a tower and went down flights of stairs to a landing that led to another hall. They followed that to a great room, a fireplace at one end, windows along the right wall, and a table in the middle set for supper.

At the head of the table was an elf, dressed all in black. On his right was Nethene and on his left, Cienno. Delia felt the hairs on her arms stand up. This could not be good.

CHAPTER 26

Delia traded a glance with Kaya and approached the table.

"Welcome, niece." The man at the head of the table rose and gave a small bow. "How nice to finally meet you." He motioned to the table where two empty places were set. "Join us."

Iyuno! Nethene and Ceinno accompanied him.

Delia didn't want to sit with these elves. There was no need to switch to her magical sight to see their auras; she could feel the evil permeating the room. Despite that, her stomach growled, betraying her to her great-uncle. She sat in the indicated chair as he smiled at her. Kaya sat beside her.

"Isn't this nice." Iyuno sat back down. More black elves appeared, carrying plates of food. They placed them in front of each elf then left the room.

Delia's stomach growled again at the aroma of the food in front of her. Some sort of roast meat alongside of root vegetables, and gravy over all. She looked up from her plate to her uncle. "Why are we here?"

Another smile spread across his face. "Why, niece! To

meet you, of course. I never understood why your father sent you away. And to humans?" He shook his head. "A trial for you, I'm sure."

Nethene and Ceinno both sneered at her. She could feel her skin crawl. "I survived."

At that the three elves laughed. "Indeed, niece. Indeed. I hear you've learned to use your magic quite well since you've returned."

She could feel her hand forming a ball of fire. Delia quickly shook it away. "Well enough."

Iyuno picked up his fork and knife and cut into his roast. "Please, eat."

She traded a glance with Kaya, who shrugged. Delia nodded and picked up her fork. The others had already begun. Would her uncle poison her? She didn't know but she was famished and decided to eat. She stabbed a piece of potato and put it in her mouth, hardly chewing before she swallowed it. If it was poisoned, would she taste it? Would it kill immediately? Before she could think about it anymore, she cut a piece of the roast and ate that. Kaya followed suit.

Delia ate quickly as the three elves made small talk. They never once mentioned the battle that had raged outside of the castle. "What happened to my father?"

Iyuno put down his cutlery. "Happened?"

"The battle. What happened?"

Her uncle chuckled. "Nothing happened. Nothing at all."

Infuriated, Delia looked at Kaya. She shook her head. Delia turned back to her uncle. "There was a battle. What happened?"

"Oh, that." Iyuno picked up his goblet of wine and sipped as Nethene and Ceinno chuckled. "We won."

Delia froze. Her father was dead? How else would this evil monster be sitting here? She picked up her goblet. It was water. She drank it all then placed the goblet carefully on the table. Was he playing a game with her? Kaya reached out and put her hand on Delia's shoulder. Delia blinked back tears. She wasn't going to believe Iyuno. "Then you have no reason to hold us. Let us go."

"I think not." Iyuno's voice was cold. "No. You'll stay with me." He raised his hand. Three black elves appeared at the door she'd come through. "Take them to their room."

Delia and Kaya rose and went with the elves. She briefly thought about using her repeller or the heat blast but how would they get out of the castle? The black-clad elves led them in a different direction from before dinner, and stopped at a furnished room this time. They were locked in, and with her magical sight, Delia could see a protection barrier put up on the door. The windows, too, were protected. There were two beds, with night clothes for them laid out on each. A glowing orb lighted the room.

Delia went to one of the glassed windows and looked out. There was a crescent moon, low in the sky, but she couldn't see much else in the dark. She wrapped her arms around herself. *What had happened?*

Kaya stepped beside her. "He's lying, you know."

Delia nodded. "Yes. But about what? He's sitting in his castle with his two favorite followers having a quiet dinner. None of them were injured. They must have come in through one of the hidden tunnels after their escape. Ugh. At best the fight was a draw and Father retreated to our camp to regroup. At worst, he's dead and the army is scattered. Iyuno could be the new king, for all we know."

"Or your father defeated the black elves and Iyuno has retreated into this castle. A prisoner. Your father doesn't know we've been captured."

Delia pressed her fingertips to her temples. "Then he's worried sick about where we are."

"Perhaps. Or perhaps Iyuno sent him a message saying he has you."

"That's not better, Kaya." Delia pounded fists on her thighs. "Not better at all."

"No, it's not."

"I should have blasted them." Delia shook her head, shoulders slumped. "I have a heat blast. And I can repel people." She pounded her fists again. "Even the sleeping spell."

Kaya put an arm around her friend's shoulders. "I thought of that too, but what then? Race through the castle like rats? Just to be recaptured?" She shook her head. "I made the same decision you did. Until we know more, we keep our powers to ourselves. Let's clean up. They left us a pitcher of water and washcloths. We'll get some sleep and make a plan in the morning."

Delia nodded.

In bed, with the glowing orb she still thought of as "magical light" turned off, she wondered at her uncle's use of torches. The magical lights were so much cleaner. Then her mind drifted to what her father was doing. If he wasn't dead already. Those thoughts churned for a long time. She didn't know when she drifted off, but woke to sunshine streaming through the windows and a black elf leaving a breakfast tray. Kaya was already up and dressed, watching the elf as he left.

After the door locked she turned to Delia. "You're awake. Good. Breakfast is served."

"Sorry I slept so late. I had a hard time getting to sleep." Delia tossed her blankets aside and got up.

"I know. I could hear you thrashing around."

"I'm sorry I kept you awake." Delia splashed her face in the remaining wash water and got dressed.

"No matter." Kaya examined the tray. "A pitcher of water, bread, cheese and apples. Not bad." She plated the food and sat down at the table. "A little butter for the bread would have been nice." Kaya ripped a roll in half and pulled a bite off, pairing it with a bit of cheese before eating it.

Delia joined her at the table. "I suppose if he didn't poison us last night he wouldn't poison us this morning."

Kaya laughed. "Probably not."

They ate companionably, in silence, until the food was gone. Kaya leaned back in the chair, mug of water in hand. "So, what's our plan?"

Delia shook her head. "We can try and break the spell on the door and sneak out."

"Not sure how that differs from knocking out our escorts last night but it's daylight now. And, without the escorts, we may have a better chance. So, sounds good to me. Let's give it a try."

CHAPTER 27

D elia brushed her hands off over the plate and walked over to stand in front of the door. Kaya did the same and stood beside her.

"So yesterday, I was blasting the castle gate but needed a shield to protect against a backlash, so I stopped to build a shield and you did your best to hold the blast. That didn't work, or we wouldn't be in this mess. I suggest you build a shield and I attack the door." Delia glanced at her friend.

Kaya nodded. "I agree." She drew a deep breath and held out her hands. "I'm ready."

Delia could feel her hands sweat. She brushed them off on her pant legs and took her own deep breath, turning on her magical sight. The yellow lines were there, same as on the gate. Would Iyuno build as strong a protection spell on this interior door as on the castle gate? Nothing to do but find out.

She raised her hands and used the spell Kaepli had taught them. "It's still not right. Same as yesterday. I need to modify it. I'm not sure how."

"You're so strong I forget you're new to magic." Kaya nodded. "Inch your spell one direction or another. That's what

Master Kaepli taught us. As a mage, we'd have to do just that, discover how to make or break a spell. This is that time."

Delia nodded, but she had no confidence in her ability to do what Kaya said. *How do I move the spell one way or another?* She tried adding a color to her spell, like an aura, but aside from a spark or two, nothing happened.

"You can do it, Delia," Kaya encouraged her.

Delia could feel her breath tremble with the effort. Master Kaepli had made it look so easy. She tried applying more power, but other than her magical force increasing in brightness, that didn't work either. She could feel drops of sweat start to trickle down her temples. What else could she do?

She heard voices on the other side of the door. "They've heard us, somehow."

"To be expected. We're generating a lot of power. One of them was sure to notice."

Delia continued. What did Kaya mean by inch the spell? Actual movement? Despite the noise from the hall, she decided to try and move one of the spell threads. She picked one at the center and eased it out of the golden lines. Her green spell began to vibrate.

"That might be it, Delia. Keep going."

Delia took another ragged breath. This was harder to do than anything she'd done before. She moved another thread, then another. She panted with the effort, but she could see the golden lines begin to vibrate as well. She was on the right track! Delia had begun to move another of her threads when she and Kaya were knocked across the room with a magical blast. They landed against the wall. Delia felt like soggy bread as three of the black elves burst into the room, Nethene behind them. He stared at them as Delia helped Kaya to her feet.

Nethene tucked his hands into the wide sleeves of his robe. "I told Uncle you'd try to break the spell."

Delia wiped the sweat from her temples. "You didn't think we'd just docilely wait here, did you?" Her words sounded more defiant than she felt.

Nethene snorted. "Of course not. I expected you to try something. Now we'll have to separate you. A bother for us," he sneered, "unpleasant for you." He waved his hand. Three more elves came into the room. "Take them to the cells."

"No!" Delia cried out. Her fear of being enslaved again washed over her like a sandstorm. She could feel herself shaking with it, terror consuming all reason.

Kaya raised her chin. "You will not win, traitor."

Nethene laughed as the black elves led them away.

Delia did her best to pull herself together as she was led down and down within the castle. She ended up in a subterranean cell, no windows, and with only one of the magic lights she had found in her father's palace. At least she wasn't in total darkness. She had no way of knowing where Kaya had been put. There was a straw pallet on a rope and wooden bedstead with one blanket. A bucket in the corner served as the toilet and a rickety wooden stand held a pitcher with a horn mug and a round of bread. Delia lay down on the bed. She was so tired; she didn't know how she'd managed to walk all the way down here.

Tears came to her eyes and leaked down her face onto the rough mattress. She already missed Kaya. What was Iyuno's plan? Was she to be traded somehow? What about Kaya? She dashed the tears away, a sudden anger filling her. Was this what she was now? A pawn? It was worse than when she was a slave. At least there she'd had some freedom of movement, of thought. The tears came again, and she cried herself to sleep.

CHAPTER 28

S he woke at a noise. It surprised her how quiet it was in this dungeon. No outside sound at all, until now. A thud out in the hallway. Delia sat up and waited. The sound of a key in the lock made scraping noises, then the door opened. A black elf with a torch—she still didn't understand why, when they had magical lights—stepped into the room, followed by another, and a third remained in the hall.

"Come," the one without the torch said. It was the same unpleasant tone as they'd used the night before. Was it night? Had she slept away the entire day? She rose and stepped to the door. She wished she'd had time to at least splash her face. It felt sticky from her dried tears. No matter, no one was going to look good after spending the day in a dark hole.

Again, she was led to the dining room. Again, Nethene, Ceinno and Iyuno were already seated, each enjoying fine glasses of red wine while they waited. Iyuno waved her to a chair. Just as Delia was seated, Kaya was brought in. Delia smiled with relief. Kaya didn't seem to be any worse for wear and, better, they sat her beside Delia again. The two clasped hands as they traded glances.

Delia was seated next to Ceinno again. The evil radiating off of him was palpable. It made her stomach turn.

"I'm glad to see you both well," Iyuno began. He nodded at one of the black elves, who stepped forward and poured each of the newcomers a glass of wine.

Delia picked up her water glass, draining it before putting it back on the table. Iyuno raised an eyebrow but nodded to the elf, who refilled the water.

"Your antics this morning could be heard all over the castle." Iyuno raised his wine glass to them. "Too bad they didn't work."

Delia had a moment where she wanted to retort that it had been working but Kaya grasped her hand in warning. Delia drew a deep breath and gave her friend a brief nod. "Why are we here? Are we hostages?"

Ceinno chuckled, giving Delia chills.

"No. Not exactly," Iyuno said. His voice drawled in laziness.

Delia didn't like the way he drew it out. "Then what? It's certainly not for our sparkling conversation."

It was Iyuno's turn to chuckle. "Your time with the humans has made you sarcastic. Very charming." He traded glances with Nethene.

Nethene nodded. "We are studying you. The only raven-haired elf! We want to see what you can do. I'll have to say the day was a bit of a disappointment."

Delia dug her nails into her palm to resist a retort. Beside her, Kaya drank her water with a nonchalance Delia envied. She picked up her wine and sipped, hoping she looked as uncaring as Kaya. "So sorry to underwhelm." She looked around the dining room with her magical sight. All of the doors had a fine mesh of magic over them. The black elves had dark brown auras. Iyuno, Nethene, and Ceinno's were all black. Apparently in his own company, Nethene didn't bother to project the false aura. The wine and water didn't have any magical properties. That didn't mean they weren't poisoned. Delia made a mental note to see if there was a way to see poison. If she got out of here alive, anyway. "What are you looking for?"

Nethene shrugged. "Something worthy of a prophecy."

"What do you think of my protection spell?" Iyuno leaned forward, eyes on Delia.

"It's very strong," Delia offered. "But I'm new at magic. I don't really have a frame of reference."

Iyuno looked to Kaya. "And you? You're supposed to be a mage. What is your opinion?"

"My skills tend more toward the healing arts."

Iyuno fell back into his chair. "I saw you both at the gate yesterday. Neither of you fool me. And with the door to your room this morning? I could feel the power. Who was working on the door?"

"We both were," Kaya spoke quickly. "A combined effort."

Nethene frowned. Delia could see he was skeptical. "I could feel a shield."

Delia shrugged. Kaya took a sip of her wine.

Iyuno waved to a guard. The elf left the room and shortly, several elves came in bringing plates of food. Delia's stomach growled immediately. Ceinno laughed as he placed his napkin in his lap. "The body can be such a traitor."

Delia couldn't help but blush. Kaya gave her hand a squeeze. They ate quickly. Delia still wanted to know what Iyuno was up to. When he finished his food and one of the elves took the plate away, Delia asked, "Where is my father?"

Iyuno looked toward her, picking up his wine. "He's dead."

Delia stared at him. A feeling of overwhelming grief washed through her with such speed she stopped breathing. She hadn't known him that long. The strength of the feeling surprised her. Again, Kaya squeezed her hand. Delia nodded. It was possible that if these three were in here having dinner at their leisure, that her father was dead, and his force destroyed. Tears sprang to her eyes. "You lie."

Iyuno shrugged. "We march on your father's palace now."

An instantaneous fear for her mother swept over her, replacing the grief. "Why?"

Nethene snorted again. "Iyuno is the rightful heir. The elves will proclaim it or they will die."

"Liar," Kaya called out. "Liar. Anyone can see by looking at the three of you that you are not fit to rule the kingdom.

Ceinno reached out a hand and made a grasping motion. Kaya's hand flew up to her neck. She began to turn red, choking.

"Stop it!" Delia turned on Ceinno and with a push of her hand, her repeller blast knocked him out of his seat to go sliding across the dining room floor. The black elf guards were on her in an instant, swords out. Nethene leapt from his chair and had both hands out in front of him. Delia could see the magic, all black and ugly, swirling between his hands. She raised her hand to him. She'd like nothing more than to blast him with her heat. Kaya collapsed into her chair, leaning over the table, coughing.

"Stop!" Iyuno held up a hand.

Nethene looked as though he'd been slapped, but he let the black magic die away. One of the guards helped Ceinno up. He dusted himself off and sauntered back to the table.

"You see, cousin, uncle, how powerful she is." He sat down and picked up his wine glass. "She has strength. She'd be a powerful ally."

Delia's eyes went wide. "There is no way."

Iyuno laughed. "Of course there is."

CHAPTER 29

I yuno placed his napkin on the table. "I do hope you've enjoyed your meal. It will be the last for a while." He nodded and the black elves surrounded Delia.

Her heart pounded as her hands grew slick.

"No!" Kaya leapt up.

At a simple wave of Iyuno's hand, she froze, her face in a grimace of both anger and fear.

That made Delia even more afraid. "What are you doing?"

Iyuno sniffed as both Nethene and Ceinno chuckled. "We're going to bring you over to our side."

Delia's head shook no of its own accord. "No. No I won't."

"We'll see." Iyuno nodded again and one of the black elves grabbed her arm.

Her magic exploded. The elf holding her flew back, his sword flying through the air. Delia rounded on the others, using the push she'd just hit Ceinno with on the other black elves trying to surround her.

Ceinno and Nethene slid around the table, surrounding

he,r and held her with their magic. She fought, but they held her arms to her sides, and aside from a trembling whole-body shield, she could do nothing.

Kaya was still held in stasis as they walked Delia out of the room and to the dungeon. They shoved her onto a wooden table, slanted so one end was on the floor with a small platform for her feet, and strapped her down. Helpless tears of anger and fear and frustration leaked from her eyes as they tilted the head of the table up to a forty-five-degree angle and wrapped her in a protection spell.

They laughed when they finished. "Not so much after all," Nethene said.

"It took two of you to wrestle me down here," Delia said. "And me with just a few months training."

Ceinno made a movement with his hand.

Delia strained for breath.

"Careful, little one, or I'll set the grid so small no air will get in." He waved again, and her breathing became easier.

She glared but said nothing.

Nethene turned to leave. "Sleep well. We begin in the morning."

Delia watched them leave, shutting the door, and soon, a protection spell covered it. It was dark. She tried to remember what was in the room as they forced her into it. She closed her eyes to avoid the oppressive absence of light. On the wall behind her was a table. There were things on it but she hadn't really seen them in her struggle. To her right, a stone wall, not a few feet away. On her left, she tried to remember, but nothing came to her. A larger space than on her right. In front of her was the wall with the door. No windows, though it was dark; perhaps there was one on a wall, but she just didn't see. More tears slid silently down her face, dripping into her ears or along her jawline.

She sniffed and did her best to stop crying. Her heart was still pounding from the fight and the fear. *What happened to Kaya? Is father really dead? What can mother do to defend the castle? What did Iyuno mean he can force me to turn?* Delia struggled against the straps. She could feel her wrists grow wet and slick. *Bloody,* she thought, and tried to pull her hands through the straps. It didn't work; they remained in place.

Delia grew tired from the struggle. She wasn't really standing and wasn't lying down. The board at her feet wasn't wide enough for her whole foot, just her heels and that was wearing, too. Her back began to hurt as well as her now injured wrists. She wished she could wipe her eyes and nose. Everything was a discomfort or pain.

It finally occurred to her that the protection field would hold her in place. When she tried it, it didn't shock her as other protection fields had. She closed her eyes and tried to rest, a steady drip, drip, drip, from behind her a strangely comforting sound as she fell asleep.

At the sound of the door being unlocked, she woke, her eyes gummed shut by last night's tears and sleep. She squeezed her eyelids together, then forced them apart just as the door opened. It was Ceinno and Nethene. They were followed by black elves with torches they put in brackets on the walls on each side of the bed and behind her.

Nethene clucked as he approached the table. "What's this! Blood?" He looked over her to her right wrist. "And on this side too." He shook his head. "Look Ceinno, she's damaged herself."

Ceinno shrugged. "She'll heal. But look at her face! She must have been crying all night." He laughed. "Afraid, little one? Afraid?"

If she hadn't been so thirsty she'd have spit, then thought

better of it. It wouldn't get through the protection field anyway. Then Nethene took it down.

Her eyes must have shown the surprise as Nethene chuckled. "You think we're so afraid of a child that we'd leave it up while we're standing right here?"

Her mouth was too dry to reply.

Ceinno came back to her side from behind her. He held a mug to her lips. "Drink, little one."

She tried to shake her head no but Nethene grabbed her by the hair and Ceinno forced her mouth open and poured the liquid in. Delia sputtered, water flying in every direction. It was water and she swallowed some, but there was something else in it. Metallic tasting. Ceinno laughed. "There will be more, little one. Oh yes. And you will drink."

"May you die a horrible death," Delia managed to croak out.

They both chuckled. "Excellent," Nethene said. "A good sign, there's still fight in her yet."

CHAPTER 30

There was no time to worry about Kaya or her mother that day, or the next, or the next. Thirsty, she couldn't but help drinking the metallic tasting liquid. She could tell the first day that it was making her compliant. She fought anyway.

The first day was the hardest. She tried making fireballs and sticking them to her tormenters when they neared. They responded with fireballs of their own. Soon her arms and legs were covered with burns. What of her long, black hair that they hadn't torn out, they finally shaved off. She had to endure the humiliation of her bowels releasing after so many hours on the table. They made especial remarks about that.

By day three she had to resist quietly, reserving her strength for that only. There had been no food at all and just the tainted water. She pulled strength from inside, strength she'd built up all of her childhood as a slave. She was quiet, obedient, but still, despite the drugs, her thoughts were her own.

On day four, Iyuno came to see her. He stood at the end of the table, staring. She realized as his eyebrow twitched that she must be a sight. Ravaged head, arms and legs, blood-stained hands and wrists and what skirt remained. Gaunt, she suspected, after no food. In a flash, she decided to try and change her aura, darken it, to fool him.

She'd been using her magical sight since the beginning. While she was building the darkened aura, in this lull, she realized that the fire was bending toward Iyuno. When she looked at Ceinno and Nethene, the same was happening with them to a lesser degree. Were they feeding on the energy of fire? Why hadn't she seen that before?

"You're not as pretty as you once were, niece."

She didn't answer. What was the point?

"My nephews seem to think you're more compliant." He stroked his chin, then shook his head. His eyes narrowed as he studied her.

She held the darkened aura but it was costing her what little energy she had left.

"No, you're not. You're waiting." He sighed. "Much stronger than I thought."

On either side of her the two elves began to object. Iyuno raised his hand to stop the protestations. "No. She's still stronger than you. Look at her aura." He turned and left.

It was only minutes before she had to drop the false aura. The day was particularly trying after that. When they finally left, Delia rested as best she could. Today's terror was a beating by invisible forces from face to feet. Everything hurt even more than before.

Hunger woke her after a while. They'd forgotten to take the torches! They were getting confident in her weakness.

Could she draw strength from the flame? She studied the flame nearest her. Would the protection field over her allow energy in like it did air? Delia did her best to push all thought of her pain away and concentrate on the fire. *Feel it,* she thought to herself. *Look at it, coax it to you like a shy kitten.* Delia trembled with the effort, but she could see a tiny arm of flame move toward her.

Come little flame, come. Don't be shy. You and I will be great friends. It seemed to take forever but she shoved that kind of thought away and concentrated. "Come," she whispered.

The barest thread of flame tickled the protection field. "Come," she whispered again. It flowed through the field's mesh. It touched her arm, but it wasn't hot. A warmth spread through her, making her dizzy. The aches and pains began to ease away. Ribs she hadn't realized were broken straightened, and her breathing became easier. Stronger, she called more of the flame's energy to her. When that torch burned out, she called on the next.

She could feel the space around her as she grew stronger. It felt as though she was the owner of the universe. Delia moved her sight outside the walls of the dungeon. It was nearly daybreak. Servants in the castle were beginning to stir, making the fires in the kitchen, preparing food. Her sight ranged through the castle. She could see Ceinno, a human female huddled, naked, at the foot of his bed. Nethene slept alone, but in the corner, a wretch of a boy, wrapped in a ragged blanket, whimpered in his sleep. Iyuno was in a tower room, already up and at the window, staring out at the brightening eastern sky.

Kaya was in the dungeon, a quarter of the way around the castle, chained to a wall, asleep on a pile of straw.

As the last of the torches gave up the last of its power, Delia gave a heave and the protection spell broke, along with the heavy leather straps holding her down. She surprised herself by stepping lightly from the table and to the door.

They hadn't bothered to put a protection spell on it, so she opened it and headed for Kaya.

Iyuno was sure to have felt her punch through the protection spell. She hurried along the corridor, more than surprised that there were no guards. Delia smiled. *Their mistake,* she thought. She broke the spell on Kaya's door and scurried across the dark room. Startled awake, Kaya cried out.

"Hush, it's me." Delia took the cuffs in her hands and at the elemental level, broke them from Kaya's wrists. "Hurry, we don't have much time."

Kaya moved quickly, falling behind Delia. "How'd you escape? They told me you were done."

"Their mistake. Later though. Iyuno must already know we're about."

With her sight, Delia led them on the most direct route to the back of the castle where the servants already had doors open to the morning air.

She could hear Iyuno calling out. "They know. Hurry."

Along the way, any torch she found she drained quickly, though they were few and far between. They burst into the kitchens. Servants ran out of the way, screaming.

Delia said, "Hurry, the black elves are on their way."

"How…" Kaya started.

"Later. Hurry."

They ran out into a small courtyard. Delia spied the small gate to the outside, a sleepy elf standing guard. "Come!"

She ran, Kaya following, hit the guard with a magic blast, and with her magic, began to raise the portcullis. The clanging and banging brought more shouts. She saw Kaya look behind her and throw a blast at the first black elf out of the kitchen door.

When the gate was four feet off of the ground, Delia charged forward, Kaya on her heels. She let the portcullis drop as soon as they passed. "We have to get into the woods and hide."

Panting, Kaya said, "That didn't work so well the last time."

"It will this time."

They covered the half mile of open land quickly, though Kaya was tiring fast. "Where?"

"There." Delia pointed into the woods. It was the wrong side of the castle from their old camp but they needed to hide first.

Into the woods, Delia led them. She held Kaya's hand and passed some of her strength to her friend. Kaya accepted it and ran.

Delia used her sight. She could see the tunnels the black elves used. *There,* she thought. *On the granite outcropping.* She pulled Kaya to a granite mound and hid behind craggy boulders. She lifted one to make an impromptu cave. They sat, out of breath, listening.

"Will this work?" Kaya asked.

"Yes," Delia whispered. "Shh." She used her sight to follow their trackers. Iyuno was so angry, she could feel him from here. Delia pulled her magic around them, making them look like granite. For hours they could hear the black elves casting back and forth. Ceinno and then Nethene rode by, berating the black elves.

By dark, the hunters had retreated to the castle. Delia pulled her magical hide down. "Let's go."

"You have strength after all of that?"

"Yes. I'll tell you how once we get farther away."

CHAPTER 31

They hustled through the woods as best they could in the dark, circling around the castle until they were headed in the direction of the camp on the road they'd come in on. "What if they aren't there?" Delia asked Kaya.

"Then we'll head home. Not much else to do if we don't know where they are." After a moment she asked, "Your strength?"

"Fire. I saw Iyuno drawing power from fire. That's why they have torches all over instead of the magic lights."

"Oh my."

"Yes. I puzzled over those torches from the first."

"You think all of his forces can do that?"

"I don't think so. Just Iyuno, Nethene and Ceinno."

They walked along in silence until they reached the spot where the camp had been. Delia looked around at the spot where her tent once stood and sighed. "It's going to be a long walk home."

"You're right." Kaya took a deep breath. "Let's walk farther tonight. I still feel too close to that castle."

Delia nodded. "Agreed."

They headed off side by side, stopping very late to sleep. They woke at dawn and continued on their way. It took ten days to get back, dodging small teams of searchers. They stopped on a hillside overlooking the valley where the palace was. "It doesn't look like it's under attack. Maybe Iyuno lied about fighting with my father. Maybe he's not dead."

"It would be just like Iyuno to tell us that. Making us grieve." Kaya crossed her arms. "Let's go. I'm looking forward to something to eat besides berries."

Delia laughed. "And just splashing my face in cold streams."

As they approached the gate, Delia felt as though something was off. "The gate is shut. Why would that be?"

Kaya shook her head. "I don't know. It's always open during the day."

Switching to her magical sight, Delia gasped. "It has a protection spell over it. I can't feel anyone inside!"

"Oh no," Kaya said. She grabbed Delia's arm. "Don't go any closer."

"What happened here?"

"No idea." Kaya turned to leave. "We can't stay here."

"Where did everyone go?" Delia felt crushed. She so wanted to find her mother, take a bath, eat, and she wasn't sure in what order.

"We'll go to my family's home."

Delia nodded, fighting back her tears. "Of course."

She followed Kaya back down the road. Her feet hurt and she was hungry, and worse, she didn't know if her parents were alive or dead. And what about Mage Kaepli and Sisruo? The tears leaked down her face.

Kaya put an arm around her shoulders. "We'll figure it out, Delia."

Delia nodded, but at the moment, she just felt exhausted.

It was another five days before they reached Kaya's home. Even in her exhaustion and hunger, Delia was amazed at the woodland setting that Kaya called home. The house was in a huge tree. They climbed up stairs that wound around the trunk until they reached a platform. Kaya opened the door to the house. "Mother! Father!"

A dog came running, its whole body gyrating in welcome. Kaya squatted down to greet the dog. "Sandy, Sandy. Hello, girl. Hello!"

"Kaya!" An elf appeared in the doorway across the room.

"Mother!" Kaya left the dog and hurried across the room. She embraced her mother in a bear hug. "I'm so happy to see you."

The two hugged and hugged, finally separating. "This is my friend, Princess Delia. Delia, this is my mother, Phara."

Delia stepped forward extending her hand. She felt shy, especially about her ruined hair, and a little out of place. Phara wrapped her arms around Delia. "Welcome. Welcome."

When Phara finally let her loose, Delia had to sniff back tears. "Thank you for the warm welcome."

Phara looked at both of them. "We heard you were captured or lost."

"We were captured, Mother. But can we tell the tale later? We're starved."

"Of course. Of course, how silly of me. Come. We'll get you something quick, then you can bathe and we'll eat again. Your father is out in the forest." She patted Kaya's arm. "He'll be so happy to see you."

After a quick snack of bread and cheese, they bathed, and Kaya loaned Delia a dress and scarf. Delia wrapped the scarf around her head to hide the stubble of her hair. They finished at supper-time and Kaya led Delia to the dining room. There they found Kaya's father.

"Father!" Kaya dashed across the room and in a repeat of earlier with her mother, embraced him in a huge hug.

She introduced Delia. "My father, Aduello."

He shook Delia's hand, clasping hers in both of his. "Welcome. Thank you for bringing our daughter home."

Delia could only nod, she was so overcome with the warmth of her welcome.

"Sit, please. Your mother is bringing out dinner."

They sat, and he poured them each a glass of wine, just as Phara brought in a platter of roasted venison and vegetables. "There. Eat until you're full." She beamed at the two of them.

Delia could hardly restrain herself as she loaded her plate with meat and vegetables.

Phara left and returned with a bowl of gravy. "This should help."

Delia poured a generous amount on her food and passed it to Kaya. "Thank you so much. It's been a very hungry fortnight."

After dinner, they retired to a study. There, Aduello poured more wine and they all sat in front of the fireplace. "Are you ready to tell your tale?"

"We are," Kaya said. She related the whole story to her parents and when she finished, both of her parent's faces were full of worry. "But what happened to the king and the palace? Do you know?"

Aduello shook his head. "We know the king left the battle at Iyuno's castle, but the entire army and the king just disappeared. The palace was attacked by Iyuno's forces, but no word has come about what happened. And you say there's a spell over the palace." He sat back in his armchair and sighed.

Delia didn't know what to think. "No one returned from the battle and no one escaped from the palace? Are they still in there? Frozen or worse?"

Phara shrugged. "We just don't know."

Delia rubbed her finger at the spot between her eyes. "I'm too tired to think."

Phara and Aduello rose. "We've kept you up too long. Rest. We'll figure this out in the morning."

Delia stood. "Thank you for taking me in."

Phara gave her a hug. "Don't be silly. We welcome you."

In her room, Delia climbed into bed in her borrowed nightgown and stared at the ceiling. What happened? Were her parents alive or not?

CHAPTER 32

Dappled sunlight, tinted green after shining through the leaves of the tree, danced on the wall opposite the bed. Delia was so comfortable she simply lay and watched the light. It was the smell of bacon that lured her out of bed. She dressed after splashing her face and went down to the kitchen.

There she found Phara, Aduello, and Kaya at the kitchen table, mugs of tea in front of each. Delia had to smile at Sandy, the dog, who had her head on Kaya's knee. "Did you sleep well?" Kaya asked.

"Yes. Thank you. I don't think I moved all night."

"Please sit," Phara said as she stood up. "I'll get you some tea. Breakfast is almost ready."

Delia chuckled. "The smell of bacon was the only thing that could get me up."

Everyone smiled. "I felt the same way," Kaya said and sipped her tea.

Breakfast was friendly, and Delia and Kaya insisted on doing the cleaning up. Phara finally relented when Delia and Kaya shooed her out of the kitchen. It didn't take them long to finish, and they found Kaya's parents in the library.

"Good. You're done," Aduello said. He closed the book he was reading. "I've been giving your father, the king, some thought, Delia."

Phara motioned to the chairs. "Please sit."

"What have you been thinking?" Delia asked.

Sandy got up from under Aduello's desk to get an ear rub from Kaya, then lay down at her feet.

"King Ucheni had fallen back from the fight at Iyuno's castle. That much I know. I also know that Iyuno attacked the palace." Aduello scratched his chin. "My theory is that Iyuno's forces harried the king all the way back. The question now is, where is the king?"

Delia nodded, her hands twisting in her lap. "And why is a protection spell over the palace?"

"Tell us about this protection spell," Phara asked. "I'm not familiar with it."

"We weren't either, Mother." Kaya leaned down to pet Sandy and was rewarded with a tail thump on the floor. "It was something Iyuno had done. Master Kaepli figured it out and had us all practice building it and taking it down." She nodded at Delia. "Princess Delia was the strongest of us at it. She was the one at the gate, with me, trying to take it down. Then the black elves began erupting from hidden tunnels and we were cut off from the army. I had been knocked silly when the protection spell whipped back on us. Delia got us away but more of the black elves came from another tunnel and captured us." She sighed. "If I hadn't been so weak, Delia could have gotten away."

Delia shook her head. "I don't think so. Iyuno had it all planned out. I was going to get captured or killed, one way or the other."

Kaya gave Delia a smile of gratitude. "Perhaps."

"What are black elves?" Aduello asked.

"Oh. That's what we called the elves following Iyuno because they all wear black," Delia said. "Iyuno and Iyuno's nephews, Ceinno, and Nethene, are all very powerful and I figured out why. That's how we escaped."

Aduello and Phara leaned forward. "Do tell."

"They can draw power from fire." Delia clasped her hands. "I had wondered why they didn't use the magical orb lights like we did. They had torches all over the castle. The magic lights are so much cleaner and safer, I didn't understand why they didn't use them. Then the day before I broke out, I saw Iyuno with my magic sight, and power was flowing from the torch to him. Then they made a mistake and didn't take the torches with them that night. I pulled power from all of the torches they'd left until I could break my bonds and get free."

Phara's eyes were wide. She looked at her husband. "Did you know this?"

He shook his head. "No. But that was a remarkable escape."

Kaya nodded. "She came and got me, and we got out. Neither of us think that the other black elves can pull power from fire. Just the two nephews and Iyuno. And now Delia."

Delia smiled her gratitude at Kaya. "I think I want to go back to father's palace and break that protection spell."

Aduello nodded thoughtfully. "I can see where that makes sense."

"But won't it whip back on you like at Iyuno's?" Kaya asked.

Delia shook her head. "I'll build a bonfire and have a lot more power than we did the last time. I have to know what's in the palace."

"Do you think your parents are in there?" Kaya looked at her friend, concern showing in her face.

"Perhaps." Delia shrugged. "Perhaps no one is there and Iyuno put the spell up as an annoyance. I don't know. But it's a first step."

Aduello nodded. "I'll send some pigeons out with a question, 'Where's Ucheni?' We could hear back within a few days."

Delia pressed her lips together. "Good. We have a plan. May I borrow a horse?"

"Of course. I'll go with you," Aduello said.

"You're not leaving me behind. I can help," Kaya said as she stood up.

"I'll pack you some food," Phara said. "And stay here to receive the pigeons."

Delia smiled. "You are all so kind." She felt a little weepy and sniffed back tears. "Thank you."

Kaya placed a hand on Delia's shoulder. "You're my friend. What else can we do?"

CHAPTER 33

They took the rest of the day to prepare and send out the pigeons. The next morning, Delia put on her own clothes, which Phara had washed and repaired. Phara made them a big breakfast and then went out with them to saddle up the horses.

"Be careful," Phara said as they settled into the saddles. "Come home to me."

"We will," Aduello told her.

Kaya blew her a kiss. "Stay well, Mother."

Phara blew one back. "You as well. And you, Delia."

"Thank you."

Aduello kicked his horse forward. Kaya and Delia did the same. Delia waved to Phara, then settled into the ride. The trip took just two days. Much better, Delia thought, than the five-day slog to Aduello's.

They made camp in front of the gate. After they had supper, Aduello stood, staring at the gate. "The spell is very complicated."

Delia stood beside him. "Yes. And strong. It took both Kaya and I to work on the one at Iyuno's."

"Before you knew about fire."

She nodded. "Yes. Tomorrow will be interesting."

In the morning they packed everything onto the horses and Kaya led them up the road a little way and hobbled them so they could graze. When she returned, Delia and Aduello were building up the campfire. They all brought wood from the forest and threw it on until it was taller than Aduello

"That should be enough," Delia told them as she brushed her hands off. She took a sip of water and stared at the gate then sighed. "Time to do this. Kaya, build a shield around us, please."

Kaya nodded and began to mutter under her breath.

"What shall I do?" Aduello asked.

"Keep watch. We're going to be focused on the protection spell. I don't want anyone sneaking up on us."

He nodded.

Delia took a breath and looked at the fire. She urged the fire to come to her, just like she did at Iyuno's. The warm glow reached her, and she began to feel stronger. *More, more,* she thought. The fire filled her. She felt invincible. Maintaining the connection with the fire, she turned to face the gate. Kaya had the shield up, large enough to cover all three of them. "I'm starting."

She raised her hands and using a spell slightly different that the one the Mage taught her, began to try and take down the protection spell. It was hard, and a trickle of sweat rolled down her temple and another down her spine.

"You're doing it, Delia! Keep it up," Kaya said.

The yellow tendrils were unravelling but there was a long way to go. She wondered if she'd have to take out every single tendril. The gate was nearly clear, but she wanted the whole spell removed.

"The fire is going out," Aduello told her.

"I don't know how long this is going to take. Can you find more wood?"

"I'll go now." He hurried off.

Delia kept working. More and more of the yellow tendrils disappeared.

Aduello came back and threw more branches on the fire. He stood beside Kaya. "Shouldn't it break soon?"

"We don't know, Father. The last one blew back on us."

"I can feel it weakening," Delia said. "But it's putting up a fight, just like last time."

"Shield is ready," Kaya said.

Delia pulled as much power as she could from the fire. Sweat dripped from her chin as she took more and more of the yellow tendrils out. She could feel the protection spell tremble. "Get ready!"

Just as she yelled the words, the protection spell snapped. The shield Kaya made protected them from most of the blast but still they were all knocked down. Kaya lost the shield spell. Delia lay on the dirt of the road, eyes closed.

"Are you all right?" Kaya hurried to Delia.

"Yes. Just resting." She opened her eyes and rolled to her feet. "Aduello? Are you all right?"

"Yes. Fine." He got up. "That's quite the blast."

Delia dusted off the back of her trousers and shirt. "Well. Let's take a look, shall we?"

Aduello and Delia kicked dirt over the remains of the fire while Kaya went for the horses. By the time she got back, the fire was out and the rocks of the fire ring were kicked back to the side of the road.

They mounted up and rode inside.

CHAPTER 34

Inside the gate, Delia saw the empty courtyard. Normally this space would be bustling, even with the army gone. Now, there was no activity except a couple of leaves drifting across the paved yard in the slight breeze. They put the horses in the empty stable, in itself a troubling sign, and proceeded to the palace.

No one was inside. Delia checked the kitchen, the great hall, and both of her parent's rooms. She stood in front of her mother's dressing table and surveyed the room. "I don't understand. Everything is in its place. There's no sign of any struggle anywhere in the palace. But no one is here."

Kaya put an arm around Delia's shoulders. "Should we check the Mage's rooms?"

Delia sighed. "I don't expect to find anything different there. But we should check."

The three left and stopped outside the workshop door. Kaya drew a deep breath and opened the door. The three went in. It was the same as in the palace. Everything in its place. "I've been using my magical sight," Delia said as she brushed her hand across the table where she'd studied. "There's nothing. No spells lingering around. Nothing to indicate where everyone went." She looked at Aduello. "That's not usual, is it? For every single elf in the palace to just leave?"

Aduello shook his head. "Not that I've ever heard. Ever. Even if the king and queen were travelling to another castle, there'd still be caretakers left behind. Spare horses. Guards." He rubbed his chin and looked around the workshop. "I have no idea."

"Let's go back to the kitchen. We didn't check for food. If there's something here, let's eat and think about this."

They left, Kaya pulling the door shut gently, and went to the kitchen. The cupboards contained only dry sausage and cheese. The fireplace had been swept clean. Rodent droppings decked the counters and table.

Kaya cleaned the table while Delia sliced sausage and cheese for each of them. Aduello pulled plates from the cupboard and drew water for them to drink. They sat at the table and ate, saying nothing.

Delia felt as though her heart had been squeezed. She'd only just reunited with her parents. Now they were gone. She was surprised when a tear fell on her hand.

Kaya reached out and patted it. "I'm sorry, Delia."

Delia nodded and sniffed, reaching up with her other hand to dash away the tears. "This is unbelievable. Where could everyone have gone? Did Iyuno do this?"

Aduello shook his head. "Over a hundred people live and work here. Even more come on business or to visit. Someone must know something about where they went. Perhaps the queen sent everyone away because Iyuno was going to attack."

"There's no sign of damage, though," Delia said, sniffing again. "If he attacked, wouldn't there be some damage? Bodies? Broken equipment?"

"There is that," Aduello said. "You're right."

"Maybe he came. Saw the palace was empty and put the protection spell up out of spite." Kaya patted Delia's hand. "He's mean enough to do that."

"Yes. But he wants to be king." Delia squeezed Kaya's hand, then reached for her water. "Wouldn't he move in right away?" She drank and put the mug down.

Aduello scratched his head. "A good point, unless he was still chasing your father. If the king wasn't here, then he'd have to chase after him. He wouldn't want your father to gather another force and return."

Delia leaned forward, elbows on the table, and rubbed her face with both hands. "We don't have enough information. We should close up the palace and go back to your home. Perhaps the pigeons will have returned with clues."

Kaya nodded. "I think that's a good idea. Would you like to get some of your own things before we go?"

Delia pushed away from the table. "Good idea."

"We'll clean up while you go," Aduello said, standing up.

Delia went to her rooms, a little spooked at the sounds of her footsteps echoing in the halls. She selected another travelling outfit, a comb—though it would be a long time before she would have enough hair to bother with—and other essentials, and stuffed them into a spare saddlebag. She went to her dresser and opened her jewelry box. There wasn't much in there. Just a few coins and a couple of necklaces and bracelets she'd brought with her, and others her mother gave her. She scooped it all up and dropped them into a pouch. She needed some way to pay others. She couldn't keep depending entirely on the generosity of others. Delia put the lid down and stuffed the pouch into a pocket. Perhaps there was a strong room in the palace where there was more coin, but she'd never asked about it and no one had thought to talk to her about it. What she had would have to do.

Back in the kitchen, the others were ready to go. "I packed the rest of the sausage and cheese," Kaya told her. "It seemed wasteful to leave it for the rodents."

They walked out to the stables and saddled their horses. Aduello cleaned up after the animals and shut the doors after Delia led the horses out. Delia closed the gates to the palace and looked up at them. "I'm going to set a protection spell," she said after a moment. "To keep others out."

She set the spell and mounted her horse. "Maybe that's what happened." She studied her work with her magical sight. "Perhaps Mage Kaepli set the spell, so the palace would stay safe when they left."

"A hopeful thought, Princess." Aduello turned his horse. "Let's hurry home and see what news has arrived."

The three rode off at a fast pace. By riding long into the night, they were back at the treehouse in a day and a half.

Phara hugged them all. "There's news."

CHAPTER 35

Delia froze. "Bad news?"

Phara shrugged. "A little of both. Let's let you clean up and eat, then we'll talk."

Delia and Kara exchanged glances. The way Phara had spoken sounded like the news was too bad to talk about. "As you wish," Delia said.

She and Kara grabbed their saddlebags and went inside and took turns at the bath, then, dressed and ready, went to the kitchen.

Phara was standing at the fireplace, stirring a pot. Aduella was at the table, a mug of tea steaming in front of him.

"The horses are taken care of." Aduella sipped his tea.

"I've made stew." Phara tapped the spoon on the side of the hanging pot and put it on the spoonrest. "It'll be ready soon if you'd like to set the table."

Delia went for the silverware while Kaya got the bowls. Phara cut slices out of a loaf of bread as Aduella got a crock of butter from the cool box. Table set, Delia, Kaya, and Aduella sat down. Phara scooped stew into a tureen and brought it to the table. "There. Let's get you all fed. You rode hard if you only took a day and a half."

Delia's stomach growled in answer. Despite her fear of Phara's news, she laughed with everyone else. It didn't take long to eat, or to clean up, either. They met in the library and settled in, goblets of wine in each hand. Delia sat on the edge of her chair, expecting the worse.

"We had all but two pigeons return. Most of the answers were that they didn't know where Ucheni was. Some offered rumors." She looked at all of them. "One, from Lord Rado, said he'd helped King Ucheni with warriors and supplies two weeks ago."

Delia looked around at the surprised faces. She knew so little about the elven kingdom. "Who's Lord Rado?"

Aduello had fallen back into his chair. "Lord Rado holds a castle on the far western border." He shook his head. "Why was the king so far west?"

"No word of the queen?" Delia twisted the goblet around and around in her hands.

"None so far. The two missing pigeons were to Sochiro Yarami, who lives to the far south, and Lady Jaizana Dedalia." Phara looked at Delia with concern. "She lives east, near the desert. It's possible the pigeons never made it to either place. Or they made it and were sent back but didn't make it here. Or," Phara paused, "they're still there and haven't been sent with a message, for whatever reasons."

Delia sipped her wine. It was a dark red, the full-bodied smoky, fruity flavor filled her mouth. "Perhaps Mother is at one of those places, hiding. That's why no one has news."

"It's possible," Aduello said. "How can we find out where they all are?"

Kaya spoke up. "Let me try scrying."

"Don't you need a special bowl or something?" Delia asked.

Kaya shook her head. "It helps to have a bowl that's been used for scrying before, but it can be done in anything that can hold water, or a still pool." She licked her lips. "I cannot guarantee anything. Scrying isn't my strong suit. I have to be able to do it to pass my Master's exam, but it's not my strongest skill."

That brought the memory of Sisruo to Delia's mind. He was supposed to take the Master's exam soon. Was he still alive to do so? She missed his silly grin. "You won't get hurt, will you?"

"No." Kaya shook her head. "But I may not see anything."

Phara looked relieved. "What do you need?"

Kaya thought a moment. "A large, wide silver bowl would be best. Failing that, a wooden bowl."

Phara looked disappointed. "I don't have a silver bowl of any sort." She thought a moment. "I have a large wooden bowl I use for greens. Will that work?"

Kaya nodded. "I can make that work, I think." She blew out a deep breath. "I'll have to prepare the bowl and myself. I'll try at dusk. The beginning and ending of a day are when the ether is thinnest." She stood up. "Let's get the bowl, mother."

The two walked back to the kitchen. Delia sat back in the chair, Aduello doing the same in his. All she could think about was where her parents were. Where was Mage Kaepli and Sisruo? She sipped her wine and wondered how Kaya would fare. She hoped Kaya was telling the truth about not getting hurt scrying. In her limited experience, magic had a habit of blowing back on the user if they were doing things wrong.

It was getting dark when Kaya came back with her mother. Her hair was unbound and combed through. She wore a robe with no belts or bindings. "You all may come and watch, but don't talk or move. I need to concentrate."

They all left and went out and down from the tree. Kaya went to a small glade and put the bowl on the ground. She took the bucket of water from Aduello and poured the liquid into the bowl. Then she knelt beside the bowl and took a breath before beginning to chant.

Delia made herself comfortable, and waited beside Phara and Aduello. Kaya's chanting was low, slow, soothing, actually. The evening birdsong decreased as the daylight faded. A soft breeze wafted by, rustling the leaves. The quiet chanting with the dying light and sound made Delia sleepy.

She woke, standing, with Kaya's hand on her shoulder. "Delia?"

Delia blinked. "What happened? Did I miss your scrying?"

Kaya chuckled. "You didn't miss much. I didn't see anything. But you!"

Delia looked at Aduello and Phara, standing on each side of her. "What?"

Phara reached out a comforting hand. "You spoke. You gave us both your mother's and your father's locations."

Delia found that hard to believe. "How?"

Kaya nodded. "I've read that it can happen. You were tired. My chanting and the evenfall relaxed you. You are part of prophecy. So, prophecy is helping, apparently."

A little panic-stricken, Delia shook her head. "I don't remember."

"That's fine. We do. You told us your mother is with Lady Dedalia and the king with Sochiro Yarami."

"Did I say where Iyuno is?"

"No." Aduello shook his head. "But we can assume he's near your father. Iyuno has to kill him before he can be king."

Delia swallowed. Full night had fallen. She felt light-headed and confused. "What do we do?"

"Your mother is safe. I think, Princess, we need to go help the king." Aduello waited.

"I feel sick, Kaya." Delia put a hand over her stomach.

"I had that reaction after my first scrying. It's normal." She turned to Phara. "We should go in. Let Delia sit down with a goblet of wine to restore her."

So, they all went in. They put Delia in front of the fire wine, and Phara went to get her a snack.

After Delia ate the fruit and cheese, she felt better. "Thank you. I was a little disoriented."

"That's fine." Phara gave her a smile. "It's hard to remember that you're new to all of this. You're taking it rather well."

Delia sighed. "Yes. I feel like I'm always running to catch up."

Aduello nodded. "Have you given thought to your decision?"

"I have." Delia drank the last of her wine. "We go to the king."

CHAPTER 36

They left the next morning after an early breakfast. The dew hadn't dried yet before they were on the road. The plan was to ride hard, to get to the king as fast as possible.

On the ride, Delia wondered what they would find when they got there. Or, just what it was she could do when they did.

The far south of the kingdom where Sochiro Yarami was a many days distant. In the evening, of the first day, Delia had Aduello tell her about both Sochiro Yarami and Lady Dedalia.

"Lady Jaizana Dedalia is an old friend of your mother's." Aduello stirred the small campfire. "She's from an old family, older than your father's, who have guarded the eastern borders for thousands of years. I believe Queen Ralae spent some time there as a young woman, learning about the area and making friends with Alia and her daughters." He sighed. "You returned to your parents via the eastern border, Princess."

Delia nodded. "I didn't see a border or guards, though."

"No. You were brought by secret elven paths. The king did try to keep your homecoming a secret."

"It didn't work." She remembered that desperate run to the palace gates. "Not his fault, I expect. Nethene's and Iyuno's spies must be everywhere, otherwise how did they know to attack us as we first approached the castle?"

"True." He drank the last of his tea. "Sochiro Yarami is like me, not a lord but the guardian of the southern borders anyway." He shook his head. "That was traditionally Iyuno's post. But when your father was crowned and Iyuno disappeared, it was given to Yarami. He's a good elf, loyal and smart. I agreed with the king that he was a good choice."

"What's on the southern border?" Delia leaned forward. If nothing else, riding around the entire elven kingdom was giving her a great insight into her land.

"We share that border with the dwarves. That region is mountainous and full of metallic ores. We have a good trade with the dwarves and it goes through the town around Yarami's castle."

Delia remembered seeing dwarves in a few of the desert towns her caravan went through, but she'd never had an opportunity to talk to them. "Do we get along?"

Aduello laughed. "As much as dwarves get along with anyone. They live nearly as long as we do and are a little sensitive, taking almost anything said to them as an affront. They're good fighters, though. We have histories of elves and dwarves fighting together against dragons and orcs."

"Orcs? I thought they were a legend."

Kaya smiled. "They may be. The last great war, even men were involved. We believe the orcs were wiped out, but no one knows. None have been seen for over a thousand years."

"Good to know. The myths made them sound evil." Delia wrapped her arms around herself and shivered. The evening had turned chill and the stories of orc's destruction were horrific.

"They were." Aduello got up and banked the fire. "That's one fight I'd rather not attend."

It took ten days to get to Yarami's town, Verda. As they entered the gates, Delia felt right at home. It was very similar to the caravan towns she'd grown up visiting. As they passed through the streets, she didn't see any particularly large group of soldiers, and none wore her father's colors. They went to an inn where the tired horses were watered, curried and led into roomy box stalls and fed. Aduello instructed the livery elf to clean all the tack, and offered him coins in advance. The elf gave a quick bow and promised it would all be cleaned by morning.

They went into the inn, where Aduello ordered two rooms and baths. Upstairs, the were given two nice rooms, both with a view of the street in front.

"We'll meet downstairs after cleaning up, and have dinner and make a plan," Aduello said.

That sounded good to Delia. After ten days of hard riding and sleeping on the ground, a nap in a soft bed sounded grand.

They gathered in the pub, ordering stew with bread and wine, and talked softly while they waited for it to arrive. A trio of dwarves sat in the back corner, while a party of five men sat under the windows. Aduello chose a table in the middle, where he could watch the door to the inn. Lowering his voice even more he said, "In the morning I'll send word to Yarami that we're here. If we can get an audience, we'll know where the king is soon enough."

Delia nodded. "Should you tell him I'm here?"

"I did think of that, but in case there's a spy, I think I'll leave that out."

Both Kaya and Delia agreed.

"I didn't notice any unusual number of soldiers as we rode in," Delia said.

"But I did notice," Kaya added, "that they seemed very alert. You've spent years in trading towns, Delia. What did you think?"

"A town's guards are always alert. Trading towns are rife with thieves and cut-purses, kidnappers and scam-artists. I'm sure Verda isn't any different. But no, I didn't think so, at least not at the time."

"Good points, both of you." Aduello stopped talking as a serving elf brought their wine.

"The food will be out in a minute," she said, then went back to the kitchen.

"And," Delia whispered as she adjusted her head scarf, "Where is Iyuno? If the king is here, shouldn't he be nearby?"

"This is a mountainous region. He could have three armies in any canyon, hidden, ready to attack at any time." Aduello sipped his wine. "We'll just have to see Yarami."

CHAPTER 37

At breakfast the next morning, Aduello sent a courier, recommended by the inn-keeper, off to the castle with a message. After they ate, they walked around the market. Delia told them about the desert caravan markets where there were stalls of exotic spices, silk, and slaves. Here it was different. There were no slaves at all, which she thoroughly approved of. Instead there were stalls with displays of ore, woolen cloth, wood, and ceramics. Both markets had money changers and grain merchants, she pointed out.

There were food vendors with foods she'd never seen. She pointed one out to Kaya. "What's that?"

Kaya grinned. "Dwarf cake. I've only ever had it once and it was delicious. Honey and nuts, flaky and light. May we get one, Father?"

He grinned too. "I believe so. It's been many years since I've tasted any, myself." He went up to the stall and ordered three from the dwarf woman running it.

She wrapped each in paper. "Three shillings."

Aduello put the coins on the counter. "Thank you." He

bowed to the proprietress and handed the cakes to Kaya and Delia. They unwrapped the cakes and walked along.

"Oh my," Delia said after the first bite. "This reminds me of the sweet cakes I had once in Encre, but better, flakier."

"Mmmm," was Kaya's response.

They washed sticky hands in the central fountain and sat on the edge, enjoying the day. It was cooler here in the mountains, but the sun was warm. Delia entertained herself by looking at the elves, men, and dwarves that walked by with her magical sight. "Everyone has an aura!"

Kaya chuckled. "Yes. Every living thing."

"The human ones don't sparkle like elven ones. The dwarves," she studied a pair of stocky ones thumping past in heavy-looking boots, "their auras, um, shimmer, I guess is the best word."

Aduello nodded. "That's why it's a shame when we go to war with each other." He looked at the sun. It's nearly midday. I'll go back to the inn and see if a message has come from the castle." He stood up and looked at Kaya. "Stay out of trouble."

Delia could see he was telling his daughter to look out for her.

"Of course, Father. No trouble at all."

He left, and Delia and Kaya stood up. "Let's check on the horses," Delia said.

"Good idea."

They went to the stable, where they said hello to the livery elf, and went to the horses. With nothing better to do, they curried the horses until their manes and tails were tangle free and their coats glistened. "We should have gotten them apples at the market," Delia said.

"Oh, that would have been a good idea. Next time." Kaya cleaned her curry brush and put it back where she found it.

Delia did the same. "I know we just had a snack, but let's go inside and get some bread and cheese. I'm hungry."

"Me, too. Days of short rations have made me famished."

The two went in and were there, finishing a plate of bread, cheese, and fruit when Aduello came in. "Glad to see you here. We have permission to see Yarami mid-afternoon." He looked around the room. There were single elves, sitting far apart in the pub, far enough away that they couldn't hear what was being said. Their eyes were on their mugs. "There's a feeling about town that I didn't notice this morning. I can't tell what it is. How long have you two been here?

Kaya and Delia traded alarmed looks. "We left the square just after you. We spent an hour grooming the horses, then came in here to eat. We've been here since." Kaya looked at Aduello. "What's wrong?"

"I don't know." He glanced at the two other elves and back to Kaya. "But something is wrong."

Delia stood up. "I'll go look at the street."

Aduello started to call her back but stopped and nodded. "See what you can."

Delia walked casually to the open door of the inn and stepped just out of the door. There was still plenty of foot-traffic. A few elves and men on horseback rode past. What might be different? No one was on the bench outside the door, so she sat down and leaned back against the wall, feet out, at ease to the casual passer-by.

It took a while to spot. She went inside. "We should go to the castle now."

Kaya and Aduello stood. He dropped coins on the table. "Let's go."

They left the inn and headed to the castle. "What did you see?" Kaya asked.

"Black auras. Not on everyone, but yesterday I didn't see any." Delia felt for the knife at her waist.

"Should we have brought our saddle bags?" Kaya asked.

"There's no time," Aduello said. "It would have looked suspicious."

Delia nodded, he was right. She did have a pang of regret for the few coins and jewelry she'd left behind. But better that than a slit throat.

They passed the market, which now seemed gray and ominous to Delia, and were not far from the castle when three elves on horseback, accompanied by four more on foot, appeared in front of them from several streets and alleys.

Aduello stopped. "Get behind me."

Delia looked over her shoulder. "There's more back here."

The three moved to stand back to back. Unbidden, a fireball formed in Delia's hand. She had no intention of being captured by black elves again. It was no matter that none of them were wearing black; she could see their auras.

Kaya readied herself as well. "I think the sleeping spell, don't you?"

Delia grinned as she squashed the fireball. "Yes. A much better idea than burning the town down."

Delia took a deep breath. She and Kaya could take out a large number of attackers quickly with the sleeping spell but what could Aduello do? Too late to ask. The black elves were attacking. She and Kaya raised their hands as one, and one black elf after another, along with their horses, slumped to the cobbled streets.

When those facing Delia were down, she turned to help Aduello. He was hard at it, using some sort of lightning to fight. Arrows whizzed past.

Delia's first job was to put the archers to sleep. Soon, Kaya was helping, but not before an arrow hit Aduello in the shoulder. He cried out in pain as Delia and Kaya put down the last archer, at their very feet.

Kaya knelt beside Aduello, who was down on one knee, his hand around the arrow. "Father. Let me see."

That was when the castle guard arrived. The Captain was on a white charger, elves in uniform before and after. "Halt!"

Delia raised her hands as the guards surrounded the three, stepping over the bodies of the black elves and horses. Kaya did the same. Aduello raised his uninjured arm.

The Captain surveyed the scene. "Explain yourselves!"

Aduello winced but replied. "I'm Aduello Herberi. I have an appointment with your Lord. We were set upon by these elves and defended ourselves."

The Captain raised an eyebrow. "You're a formidable fighting force."

"Not me so much as my daughter and," he hesitated for just a moment, "her friend."

The Captain reined in his prancing horse and sighed. "Collect all of the downed elves." He looked at Kaya and Delia. What did you do to them and their horses?"

Kaya answered. "We used our magic to put them to sleep."

He nodded. "Can you wake the horses, at least?"

"Yes, sir." Kaya looked at Delia. "But I recommend we not wake the elves until you are ready to ask them your questions. We can do that one at a time."

The Captain's eyebrow rose again. "Very well." He motioned to one of the elven guards. "Go get a wagon." The elf hurried off. "After you wake the horses, I'm going to have to secure your hands."

"But Father is injured."

"We'll deal with that." He motioned to his guards.

Two guards came to each of them and helped Kaya and her father to their feet. They let the Delia and Kaya wake the horses, then they tied their hands behind them and Aduello's to his side. They were escorted, led by the Captain, to the castle.

Delia thought this was an inauspicious way to meet the castle's lord but there was nothing she could do about it. The guards were courteous enough, but brooked no nonsense. Fair enough, she thought. They didn't know she was on their side.

All three were taken first to the healer, an elf nearly the age of Master Kaepli. After Aduello's wound was dealt with, they were taken to a clean, dry cell with three wooden chairs and a table, which was set with a pitcher of water and three wooden mugs. The door closed behind them and the lock turned.

Aduello sat down and Kaya poured him water. Delia studied the door. "There's no protection spell."

Kaya nodded. "I suspect the Captain believed us. But he's just making sure we stay put until he talks to Yarami." She poured a mug of water for herself and one for Delia, handing it to her. "The master did a good job on your shoulder, Father. I should have no trouble with healing it as we go forward." She sipped her water.

Delia sat down as well. She could sense two guards on the other side of the heavy oaken door. They would be summoned soon enough. "Well, that was a good start." She drank about half her mug of water.

Aduello nodded. "Of course, not the introduction I would have preferred." He sighed and sipped again. "But, we're not dead, so that's something. And Yarami now has prisoners to interrogate. A good thing, I think."

Kaya and Delia nodded. Then they spent the rest of the time with their own thoughts.

Delia was considering whether they could have done anything else. What if they'd just stayed at the inn? No, that wouldn't have been good. The black elves would have forced their way in. Perhaps hurt any guests and the inn-keeper and his family. That would have been a disaster. She played with the wooden mug, turning it around and around as she absently looked at the patterns in the grain.

"Aduello, you were using lightning to defend yourself. How do you…"

The key in the door lock sounded. Delia put her mug down and turned to look.

The door opened. It was the Captain of the Guard. "Come with me."

The three rose and followed the captain. Four guards followed. They traveled up and up, three flights of stairs, and were ushered into a pleasant room. Books and scrolls lined shelf upon shelf on the side walls. In front of them was a large window, an elaborately-carved desk in front of it, and a silver-haired elf sitting behind in a matching wooden, high-backed chair. The three walked to the front of the desk and waited as the elf finished with his scroll and rolled it up.

He looked at them. "Aduello Herberi, daughter Kaya, and," he studied Delia. "You must be Princess Delia."

Delia was impressed. She removed her head scarf to show him her black stubble. "Yes, Sire."

He nodded at the sight of her shorn skull. "I'm not a 'sire.' 'Lord' is the appropriate title." He motioned to the three chairs in front of the desk. "Please sit."

The three sat down on the plain wooden seats as Yarami folded his hands on the desk. The Captain of the Guard stood to the side. Delia turned to look. Two of the guards had stationed themselves on either side of the now closed door. She turned back to Yarami.

"Captain Catari told me what he found and your story. I am disturbed that these dissidents are in Verda." He sighed, and a look of regret, then resignation crossed his face. "You suspect I know where the king is."

Aduello nodded, then winced and went still. "Yes, My Lord Yarami. Princess Delia had a vision."

Yarami's eyebrow rose. "Weren't you just released from human slavery?"

Delia nodded. "Yes, My Lord. I was, just a few months ago. Apparently, I'm a fast learner."

A knock sounded at the door. One of the guards opened it. In came the healer.

"Master Juner, come in. We were just getting to our guest's abilities."

The old elf looked at Delia. "I didn't ask in the dispensary, but you're Princess Delia; am I correct?"

"Yes, Master Juner." Delia sighed. "Apparently not as inconspicuous as we'd hoped."

One of the guards brought the mage a chair. He sat down. "No. I should think not. What did you do to the elves who attacked you?"

"A sleeping spell. Kaya and I both have learned it. Master Kaepli developed it, knowing we were going after Iyuno and his forces. It's much better than killing them."

The old elf nodded. "Indeed." He looked at Yarami. "I can't wake them."

"We can. We can teach you the spell and how to wake them." Kaya offered.

The lord and the mage studied Kaya, then Delia. "An

interesting development." Lord Yarami drummed his fingers on the desk. "I accept your offer."

"Do you know where my father, King Ucheni, is?" Delia just blurt it out, then round-eyed, covered her mouth. That was too abrupt. She put her hands back in her lap, head down. She could feel a blush creep up her neck to her cheeks.

CHAPTER 38

Yarami smiled. "A good question, Princess." He took a breath. "You want to join him? You seem to have the skills to be of use."

Delia nodded. "We all do. Kaya is a great healer, Aduello is an old friend of the King. We can help."

"I believe you can. I can have someone guide you to them."

"Do you know where Iyuno and his forces are?" Aduello shifted in his chair, cradling his arm in its sling.

The mage stroked his beard. "In a canyon, playing cat and mouse with his nephew, the king." He shook his head. "It's bad business. Outposts and homesteads are being destroyed. The skirmishes spill over into the dwarves' territory and they're none too pleased about it."

Lord Yarami studied Delia. "You know about the prophecy?"

"I've been told. But I don't feel like a very powerful elf."

Yarami's eyebrow went up again. "Perhaps. But the speed with which you learn, and the number of unique powers you've learned may prove otherwise." He pushed a lock of his loose hair away from his face. "I'll send you." He looked at Aduello. "You're injured. Would you prefer to stay here?"

"My daughter is a good healer. She can tend to the wound."

Yarami nodded. "Very well. I'll send a small force with you." He looked at Captain Catari. "You've been itching to go. Set up Lieutenant Gormaldi to be the leader of the guard. Take up to ten of your best."

"I'd like to go as well, My Lord."

Yarami turned to stare at Master Juner. "And you? I didn't know you had any desire to go to battle."

"You misunderstand me, My Lord. I want to talk to Master Kaepli." He looked at Kaya and Delia. "He apparently has an amazing ability to create spells."

"Ah." Yarami smiled. "A professional curiosity." He nodded. "Very well. I know your assistants are quite capable."

"Thank you, My Lord." He gave a gentle bow from the waist.

"Go with my blessings. All of you. Tell His Majesty I'd send more elves if I had them." He looked at Delia. "But I suspect he has all the help he needs."

Delia and her companions rose, as did Master Juner. Captain Catari led them out of the room and down to the main entrance. "Do you have everything you need?" he asked.

"We don't know." Aduello adjusted the sling a little. "We abandoned everything at the inn when we realized there was trouble. Everything, including the horses, may still be there or not."

"Gallett," he called.

A young elf stepped forward. He'd been one of the elves in the Lord's office. "Sir."

"Go with them. Find out if their belongings are still intact. Bring them back if not." He turned back to Aduello. "If everything is in place, Aduello, meet me at the west gate at sunrise."

"Thank you, Captain."

The three turned to leave and the young guard followed. Aduello and Kaya walked side by side. Delia followed beside Gallett. She smiled to see that he was distressed by that. "Where are you from, Gallett?"

He looked at her, wide-eyed. "Um, nearby, Princess." He ducked his head and touched his forehead.

"No formalities with me, Gallett. Is there a title I should use with your name? Soldier, Guard?"

"No, Princess. I'm new. I don't have a rank yet. They just yell, 'Gallett!' "

She smiled. "That's what my master used to do. 'Delia!' he'd bellow when he wanted me."

He looked at her sideways. "I thought that just a story, Princess."

She sighed. "No. No story. Sixty years, close enough, I was a slave on a caravan. Back and forth, up and down through the desert, selling slaves and assorted goods for my Master."

"That's not right, Princess."

"No. But my parents, the king and queen, were trying to hide me. Now I'm back," she said in a more cheerful voice. "What about your parents?"

He sighed. "We had a homestead, to the south. I'm here because Iyuno's elves destroyed it." His voice was hard, but a tear formed and raced down his cheek. He dashed it away quickly

"I am so sorry, Gallett. Is that why you became a guard?"

"Yes, Princess. I had no one left. Even though I'm too young, Lord Yarami let me join the Guards."

"That was kind of him."

"Yes. Yes it was."

By then they were back at the inn. Everything seemed peaceful. They checked the horses first. They were in their stalls, dozing. Delia was relieved. She liked the little mare she'd been riding and had been anxious that something may have happened to her.

They went to their rooms. Nothing had been disturbed. Aduello sighed. "That's a relief." He looked at Gallett. "Tell your Captain that we are fine. We'll meet him at the west gate at dawn."

Gallett nodded, gave Delia a shy smile, and left. Aduello sat on Kaya's bed. "Let's spend the rest of the afternoon preparing. Kaya, could you take a look at my shoulder? It really hurts. Delia, could you arrange with the inn-keeper for trail food for the three of us? Five days-worth if possible. Then ask the livery elf for provisions for the horses."

He reached into a pocket and drew out a pouch. "Take this to pay." He held out several gold coins.

"I have some money. And I brought jewelry to sell. I can take care of it."

"Nonsense. The king will repay me. Trust me. Keep your things. We may have need of them later." He urged her to take the coins.

Delia didn't want to. She felt like a burden. After he shoved his hand at her again, she relented and took the coins. "Very well. I'll get everything arranged." She put the coins in her pocket and left.

The inn-keeper was agreeable to provide the food. They discussed what would be best, then Delia went to the livery elf. The same there. She paid the elf and told him when they wanted to go. He agreed to have the horses ready.

There were a few coins left. She went to the market, which was closing down, and bought six apples, three for the horses and three for them. Delia had a feeling the horses, and the elves, would need a treat before the battle began.

CHAPTER 39

The meeting at dawn at the west gate was uneventful. The night guards unbarred the town gate and let them through. They rode silently through the dawn mists. Delia pulled her cloak tighter around her. The weather was getting colder. Summer was nearly at an end and fall would arrive soon. With luck, this war would be finished soon, and she could go back to the palace and learn more about being an elf than fighting.

They rode steadily, only stopping at noonday to rest the horses and eat. Then it was back in the saddle. Delia rode beside Captain Catari after they left their lunch spot. "How long until we reach the king, Captain?"

"Another day. We'll camp tonight and begin again in the morning. It will be after dark when we arrive, even riding late into the night tonight. It seems to me speed is most important right now."

Delia agreed with him. "And Iyuno?"

"We don't know where he is, exactly. His forces are spread throughout the mountains." His look went hard. "He attacks anyone not pledged to him. We've lost many elves."

"Gallett told me about his family. I am truly sorry, Captain."

"Thank you." He looked at her. "This prophecy, do you think it will come to pass?"

Delia shook her head. "I don't know, Captain. I only heard about it when I was returned to the elves. It seems to me to be far-fetched. I've only practiced magic for a less than a handful of months. I don't see how I could be more powerful than Iyuno or his nephews. They've had decades or hundreds of years of practice and study."

"I've heard you can do some amazing things."

She shrugged. "I can throw fireballs, which isn't common, but not unusual. I can throw an invisible heat ball, kind of like a force that pushes. Master Kaepli taught me how to put an opponent to sleep, but he taught that to all of his apprentices, as well as how to build a protective wall and how to take it down. But again. He taught that to his apprentices at the same time." Delia shook her head. "No. To be honest, I don't feel special at all."

"Don't discount your abilities, Princess. I do not have those skills and neither do any of my men. Perhaps Master Juner does, but if so, he's never told me."

Captain Catari pulled away from the head of the small column and dropped back to check on the rear. Delia gave some thought to what he'd said. Perhaps it was true, then. Sisruo, Kaya, and the others were powerful elves, as was Master Kaepli but even though Kaya and her father knew about pulling power from fire, they'd never said if they'd tried it themselves. And who knew what she herself could do if pushed. Though what else could push her after being tortured for days in Iyuno's dungeon, she shuddered to think.

They made a quick stop at sundown, to let the horses graze and grab a cold bite of food for themselves, then remounted and rode into the night. It was close to midnight, Delia thought, when they finally halted for sleep. The horses were hobbled so they could graze or sleep. The elves didn't set up tents. Everyone rolled into their bedrolls and slept under the stars.

The next morning came all too soon for Delia. Cold biscuits and jerky were handed around as breakfast. Water from the stream was all there was to drink. Delia was stiff and cold from sleeping on the cold ground, and wet from the heavy dew that had fallen. She retrieved her horse and saddled the mare herself, tying the damp bedroll on the back of the saddle. *I'll take it down and spread it out to dry at noon-tide*, she thought. *That way it will be at least a little drier when I have to sleep in it tonight.*

They formed up and rode just as the sun began to brighten the eastern sky. The second day was much like the first. Delia found herself dozing in the saddle. She nearly fell off of her horse once when it stumbled. That had frightened her. Embarrassed, she looked around. Kaya and Mage Juner looked sleepy but the soldiers were alert, keeping an eye on their surroundings and talking softly to each other. The Captain was talking to his sergeant, but they were too far away for her to hear their conversation. She settled back into her saddle after patting the sure-footed horse on the neck, thankful no one had seen her near fall.

More jerky was supper when they stopped just before sunset. She pulled out the apples and handed them to Kaya and Aduello. Her horse whinnied her happiness when Delia presented the little mare with it, on the flat of her hand. She munched it messily, then leaned down to lip up the pieces she'd dropped. *A small kindness,* Delia thought as she stroked the horse's neck. A battle was coming. She could feel it, and perhaps the little mare wouldn't live through it.

They mounted up and Delia looked at the guards, Kaya, and Aduello. Perhaps none of them would live through it. She fell in beside Master Juner. "And how are you? It's been a hard ride."

He smiled at her. "It's true I'm getting old, but my strength is not diminished. Tell me about the spells Master Kaepli has taught you."

They spent many miles talking about the protective wall, the sleeping spell and much more. Delia was surprised when Captain Catari raised his hand to halt the troop.

In the dark, everyone behind her stopped because she had stopped. Was something wrong? She looked around, trying to sense trouble coming.

"We're here," he announced. "Stay while I ride ahead to announce us."

Delia breathed a sigh of relief but didn't stop trying to sense the darkness around them. Knowing her uncle, this would be when he'd attack.

For once, she was glad to be wrong. Captain Catari returned. "Forward!"

They rode into a well-guarded camp. Defensive spikes and ditches surrounded the tents. Guards were on duty, as far as Delia could tell, every thirty feet or so, with fires. Elves from the camp took the horses as the Captain, Mage Juner, Aduello, Kaya, and Delia were led to the king's tent. Even at this late hour, he was still awake. Master Kaepli was with him as well as Mysteso and Neoni, looking at maps on a table in the middle of his tent.

King Ucheni opened his arms. "Daughter, come, let me give you a hug of welcome."

Delia had tears in her eyes when he released her. "Father. I was so worried about you."

"And I you, daughter." He grinned at the others in the

tent. "Look, my daughter who was lost has been returned to me!"

After grins all around, she introduced Kaya and Aduello. The king shook both of their hands. "Thank you for keeping her safe."

"It was she who kept me safe," Kaya told him. "She arranged our escape."

Ucheni nodded. "A tale for another day, I'm afraid. You've come at a desperate time."

Delia stepped back from the map table. "How may we help, Sire?"

"Master Kaepli?" the king invited.

The mage stepped forward. "Iyuno is just about finished blocking us into this valley. But," he nodded to the king and Delia, "it's a trap of our own choosing."

Delia didn't think 'trap' was a good thing.

"We have set up hidden traps in the passages leading here. We've trained more elves in how to use the sleeping spell." He looked at Delia. "And now, we have the Princess of prophecy."

Delia blushed under everyone's stare. "And the plan, Master Kaepli?"

"We draw them down here. A challenge was issued, from His Majesty," he nodded to Ucheni, "to Iyuno."

Delia's heart sank. She knew from personal experience how powerful her uncle was. "A duel?"

The mage nodded. "We have to stop Iyuno himself. Stopping his army isn't enough."

Ucheni spoke. "My uncle has accepted. We know he'll try some trickery. We've done what we can to defend against whatever it may be. We meet tomorrow at mid-day. So. Go. Rest. The battle starts tomorrow."

CHAPTER 40

Delia saw Master Kaepli and Master Juner leave together with Kaya. Aduello followed after greeting the king as an old friend. Neoni and Mysteso took Captain Catari with them. Finally, she and the king were alone.

"How are you, father?"

He took her into another hug. "Better, now that you are here. How did you escape?"

"A long story, father. Better left for a quiet winter's night in front of the fire. But, one thing came of it, I found the key to Iyuno's and his nephew's, power. Fire."

Ucheni looked at her, puzzlement clear on his face. "Fire?"

"Yes." She looked at the lamp hanging over the map table. "Look with your magical sight."

She stared at the small flame, willing it to share its power with her. A tiny thread left the flame and came to Delia's hand. As soon as it touched her, the soreness and weariness of the last two days left her. She stopped the call there, so she wouldn't extinguish the lamp. "You see?"

The king looked at her, open mouthed. "How did you learn that?"

"I saw Iyuno do it in the dungeon."

Her father started to speak.

"For another time, father. Really. But as I realized when I was first returned to you, most elves don't use their magical sight very often. I do because it's still new to me. So, one day, he was in the dungeon, gloating, and I saw what he was doing. His black elves made a mistake. Usually they left with the torches, but one night they forgot. I took advantage and got both Kaya and myself out. Then when we got to the palace, it was protected, everyone gone. I was so worried."

"I am sorry, daughter. We needed to protect everyone. It seemed best, especially since Master Kaepli knew how to set the protection spell."

"I thought so. Anyway, Kaya and I went to her home. We arrived half-starved and bedraggled, but Aduello and his wife Phara have been wonderful. He was injured in a skirmish we had in Verda."

"I'll keep that in mind." He sighed. "Go, rest. Someone will take you to a tent." He smiled. "I'm glad you are here."

"As am I. Rest well, father."

"And you."

When she left the tent, a guard walked her to a tent set aside for her. Her saddlebags and bedroll were there, with the bedroll already spread out on a cot. She drank some water from a pitcher and mug left on a small table for her, and some bread and cheese. That at least stopped the hunger pangs enough that she could relax.

The brief burst of energy she received from the lamp fire had gone. She was just tired. She lay down, thinking about the next day, but was asleep before she could form a whole thought.

The next morning, she awoke late. She left the tent and went in search of Master Kaepli. His tent was full. Sisruo stood up when she entered, a grin spread across his face. "Princess Delia!"

She blushed as everyone turned to see her. Kaya was beaming from next to Master Kaepli. "I told you." Sisruo hovered near her and her heart beat faster at his presence. The whole group gathered around her for hugs and handshakes until Master Kaepli cleared his throat. The group settled down. Beside Kaepli was Master Juner. "Kaya was telling us about your escape. Power from fire?"

"Yes, Master. I can demonstrate, if you have a torch."

Kaepli nodded to Couran who dashed out of the open tent door. "We've been telling Master Juner about the protection spell. Kaya tells us that you broke the one at the palace."

"I did. With the help of what I'm going to show you. But tell me about this duel? What will happen?"

Master Kaepli sat down. "It's hard to know. Iyuno has the more powerful magic. Your father has his own strengths, of course. They can duel with magic, with weapons, or both. It's their choice."

That did not sound good to Delia. She knew what Iyuno could do. The fear must have shown on her face.

"Do not fear, child. While your father is keeping Iyuno busy, we'll be dealing with his army."

Her eyebrows drew together. "Doesn't that break protocol?"

"A little," the mage shrugged. "But Iyuno's conceit is so huge, he decided to accept the challenge."

"Nethene and Ceinno are very powerful. Not elves to be trifled with." Delia had a flashback to the dungeon and shivered. She shoved the memory away.

"We know. Kaya has told us." He looked at her with sympathy. "We have you."

She didn't know what to say to that. Everyone was putting entirely too much faith in her new powers, as far as she was concerned. That was when Couran came back with a torch. He stood in the middle of the tent.

"Go ahead," Kaepli said.

Delia took a breath and held out her hand. It was harder to see in the daylight but everyone in the tent gasped when a small tendril of fire power reached her fingertips. Like it did last night, she felt better, stronger, immediately. She drained the torch of power in preparation for mid-day. "That's it. I took all the power it had."

"And what does it do to you?" Master Kaepli asked.

She told them.

Kaepli looked at Kaya. "Have you tried this?"

She nodded. "Both my father and I, after we saw what she could do. "Neither of us could do it."

Couran lit the torch. Each apprentice and Kaepli and Juner tried. They couldn't do it. "You say you broke the protection spell by using the power of a bonfire?" Kaepli asked.

"I did." Delia nodded. "The bigger the fire, the more power I can draw."

"And Iyuno, Nethene, and Ceinno can all do this?"

Kaya and Delia nodded.

Kaepli stroked his beard. "How far can you draw the power?"

"I don't know. I've only drawn from fires close to me."

Juner and Kaepli traded glances. "All of you go. Eat. You'll need your strength. Delia. If you would stay just a moment."

The rest left, Sisruo exchanging glances with her until he was out of sight.

"Have you eaten?" Kaepli asked.

"No. I slept late. The ride was very hard."

"We'll let you go in a moment." He again looked at Juner. "We think you need to know more of the prophecy."

Delia's heart raced. More? How much more could there be? It already put all of the weight of the kingdom on her shoulders. She took a stool, folding her hands in her lap. More prophecy? What now?

Kaepli cleared his throat. "We haven't told the others, though the king knows the whole prophecy. He was much encouraged when you arrived last night. We were sure Iyuno had you."

Master Juner took over. "We encouraged the king to make that challenge. The prophecy is quite clear. You will be the one to win against Iyuno."

They let that sink in.

Delia blinked. "But, the duel is between the two of them. How will that work?"

Kaepli shook his head. "That is still to be revealed. The prophesy says what happens, not how."

"That seems less than helpful. It could be today or in a hundred years." She was disgusted with the whole prophecy thing. Just because she had black hair instead of everyone else's blonde, she was the most powerful? It was just ridiculous. Delia stood up. "I'm not going to base my life on some mystical pronouncements. Father is a strong elf and can fight his own battles."

"Wait, Princess." Juner held up his hand. "The line of succession falls to you. If, and I do mean if, your father falls, you must be there to take over the duel. Otherwise Iyuno's forces will keep attacking until he's killed you or you kill him. The line is not free for him until you are dead."

The bluntness of his words gave Delia a shiver. Chased across the world by Iyuno because she was Ucheni's heir? The thought was horrifying. She sat back down. "So, I must stand by while Father duels?"

Both mages nodded. "The fight must end today."

"What about Nethene and Ceinno? They're nearly as powerful as Iyuno."

Kaepli sighed. "It is unfortunate, but they've made their stance clear. They must perish as well."

Delia rubbed an eye. More killing. More death. Wasn't there enough already? "You have a plan?"

"We think they'll each be leading an arm of Iyuno's army. We mentioned last night that we have traps in all of the approaches. Iyuno's force will be allowed into the valley with him but then all the passes will be blocked. We have men along all of the routes, ready to attack."

Delia licked her lips. The carnage would be terrifying. Her stomach rolled, making her glad she hadn't eaten anything yet. "This has to be done?"

Kaepli looked at her with a mix of kindness and sorrow. "Yes."

That seemed so final a word. *Yes. We must kill hundreds of elves.* This is not what she imagined as a slave in the caravan. Delia stood up again. "I must eat."

The mages rose and bowed. "Thank you, Princess."

She bowed and left. The sunshine outside the tent belied the dark words she'd just heard. The sky was an amethyst blue. Puffy clouds drifted across the sky in a soft, warm breeze. Birds were singing in the trees and a butterfly crossed her path, searching for an untrampled flower. Disheartened, she walked to where the cook tent should be.

There she found Sisruo, sitting at a table with a mug in front of him.

He leapt up when he saw her, but stopped as he looked into her face "What's wrong, Princess?"

He doesn't know, she thought, then schooled her face into a happier one. "The mages have been telling me the plan. It seems desperate."

"It is. But come, let me get you some food." He walked with her to the cooks, who were finishing up the service. "A bowl for the Princess, please."

The elf at the long board table nodded to the Princess and brought a bowl of mush with honey on top and a sprinkling of nuts, along with a mug of tea. He bowed as he handed it to her.

"Thank you. Very kind of you."

"Anything we can do, Princess," he said.

She nodded and walked to Sisruo's table. "We haven't had time to talk."

He nodded and waited for her to sit before he did. "True. After you left the tent, I had my own preparations to complete."

She stirred the mush around, mixing in the nuts and honey, then scooped a small spoonful and ate it. It tasted like so much sawdust in her mouth, but she knew she needed the strength, so swallowed. "Much has happened since the battle at Iyuno's castle."

Sisruo shrugged. "You've grown thinner, Princess. Great hardships have befallen you."

Delia appreciated the look of sympathy on his face. "I have. There were long, hungry days on the road. Kaya was a wonderful companion."

"She's a good elf." Sisruo took a sip of his tea. "She says the same of you, by the way."

Delia had to smile. "A bonding experience, you might say." She ate more of the mush, feeling better for the kind words Kaya had said. She took a deep breath. "And your role today?"

"I am to block Iyuno's escape. I have a small force and we'll come in behind Iyuno. At a signal from Mage Kaepli, I'll attack."

Her spoon stopped just above the bowl. "Just a small force?"

Sisruo shrugged. "He is only allowed a hundred elves. We should be fine. The sleeping spell will be the primary weapon." He tapped the sword at his hip. "But we have these as well."

"Don't forget the fireballs."

He smiled. "I won't. But I am not as good with them as you are. We'll be fine. Couran and Pelan will be with me." He brightened. "Your Captain Catari was a welcome guest. He'll be leading a group at the south pass. They left very early this morning."

Delia gave a thought for the Captain and his elves. She hoped they'd be spared today.

"Eat, Princess. We must go soon."

She nodded and spooned more into her mouth. *Too soon.*

CHAPTER 41

Sisruo had to leave, but she gave him a hug before he did. He was surprised and hugged back awkwardly, blushing the whole while, but he left grinning. She hoped she hadn't distracted him too much, with a battle yet to come. She choked down the rest of her mush and, taking the bowl to the cooks, thanked them for the food.

At her tent, laid out across her bed, was armor, and a cloak in her father's house colors. The wool of the cloak was heavy, but soft and fine. An embroidered sigil was on the right shoulder, a blue butterfly on a rose. The same sigil was on the pin to close the cloak, and on her helmet and the breastplate of the armor.

A knock on the tent pole made her turn. "Come."

Her father walked into the tent, a young female elf with him. He was dressed in armor very similar to hers, but his sigil was a bluebird on a holly branch. "Ah, you found it." He smiled. "This is Alia." The elf bowed. "She'll help you with the armor."

"I've never worn armor, Father."

"True, but this armor is enchanted. It will help protect

you." He walked over and gave her a hug. "Masters Kaepli and Juner told me they'd talked to you."

She nodded, looking up into his eyes. "They told me."

He drew a deep breath. "Alia is a good shield maiden. She'll be your right hand today. Whatever you need, tell her. She will make it happen."

Delia smiled and nodded to the elf. "Thank you." She looked back to her father. "What else can I do?"

Ucheni smiled. "Your mother will be proud of us today. Do your best. That's all anyone can ask." He leaned over and kissed her on the forehead. "Fight well." With that he turned and was out of the tent before she could say anything. She was left standing, staring after him. *He could die today,* she thought. *I've hardly had a chance to get to know him.* Tears prickled in her eyes.

"Princess. Let's get you dressed." Alia picked up a leg piece.

Delia dashed the impending tears away and shook her head. "I cannot wear all of that. I've never worn armor. I'll move too slowly."

Alia nodded and touched the tip of her tongue to her upper lip. "The breastplate then. That's where most of the protection is anyway. And the helmet and cloak. They both have magical properties as well."

Delia sighed. "Very well. As I dress, tell me what each piece is capable of."

Half an hour later, a horn sounded. Delia shrugged her shoulders. The armor was lighter on than she had supposed. The blue cloak, the color of her eyes, she realized, floated behind her, never in the way as she practiced her fighting moves. "I think this will work." She smiled at Alia. "Thank you." Delia reset the sword at her hip though she didn't think she'd use it. "Now. I'll need a huge bonfire at the dueling field. The biggest fire you can build. But it cannot be lit until I signal. I don't want Iyuno to have any advantage."

"Fire, Princess?"

"Yes. Part of my magic." Delia blinked. "And your magic?"

"I have skill with the sword, Princess. Magical skill, though I'm very good without it. And I know where my opponent will strike before it happens."

"Good skills. Can you tell of strikes for me?"

Alia cocked her head. "No one has ever asked, Princess. I do not know."

"Is it just physical weapons or can you tell when a magical strike is coming?"

"I," Alia thought for a moment. "I have no idea." Her face was crestfallen. "I'm sorry, Princess. I've never thought of it."

Delia sighed. "Well today, as I fight, see if you can tell. If I have to get into the field with Iyuno, a notice of what he intends would be helpful."

Alia nodded. Her freckles, unusual in an elf, stood out against a now pale face.

Delia patted her on the shoulder. "It's new to all of us, Alia. We'll do what we can." She spun around slowly. "Am I ready?"

"Yes, Princess." Alia went to the tent flap and held it open. "We're to assemble on the field."

Delia nodded. "Let's go, then."

They worked their way through the ranks, the elves parting to let her through. When she got to the front line, her father stood about thirty feet ahead. Iyuno's forces were on the other side, rank after rank of black. Nothing like the bright colors of her father's forces. She was surprised to see Lord Enaur next to her.

"My Lord. I didn't know you were here."

He smiled. "My king and princess are in need, Your Highness." He gave a small bow. "Where else would I be?"

"We are grateful, My Lord." She gave him a small bow then pointed with her chin to Iyuno's side of the field. "An evil sight."

Enaur chuckled. "An intimidation tactic. His army is no more powerful magically than ours. But the solid black mass makes it seem so. Iyuno and his two nephews are the power. We stop them, and the rest will disappear back into the elven population."

She hoped so.

Horns sounded. Iyuno and Ucheni began their march forward. Her father's cape was the same color as hers and looked like a piece of sky had fallen and attached itself to him.

Ten feet in front of the line, Delia saw Alia instructing the soldiers in the building of a wooden pyre. She nodded her approval. Father was correct. She was a wonderful shield maiden.

Lord Enaur noticed. "What is she doing?"

"What I asked," Delia said, then turned her attention back to her father. On the far side of the field, Delia searched for a pyre similar to hers. Her eyebrows drew together. She didn't see one. Was it behind or in the middle of his force? Was he so confident in his powers that he didn't feel the need for a fire? She shifted foot to foot, her hand tapping on her thigh. What tricks did her uncle have that she was not prepared for?

The walk to the middle seemed to take forever but finally, the two elves stopped, perhaps twenty feet apart. *Too close,* Delia thought. *Way too close.* Did her father know the sleeping spell? Damn for such a late arrival last night. She knew next to nothing about his skills. She found herself breathing too fast. Then focused on taking deep, slow breaths. It wouldn't do to hyperventilate and pass out at the front of the army.

At a signal from Kaepli, the two began with fireballs. As the fire splashed harmlessly against magical shields, Delia wondered if that was the signal for Sisruo as well. She had no time to think about it. Her father and Iyuno were circling each other. Delia held her breath.

CHAPTER 42

Her father, Delia could see, was a formidable fighter, but Iyuno, even without a fire to draw power from, was better. She found herself making tiny movements, fighting Iyuno with her father. Twice she found a fireball in her hand, ready to throw, but had to extinguish it in frustration. Ucheni was missing multiple chances to deal Iyuno a blow. As a consequence, he was falling back, step by step. She gripped and re-gripped her sword pommel until her hand hurt.

Alia approached. "The fire is ready, Princess."

Delia nodded, never taking her eyes from her father. "Can you tell what Iyuno is going to do?"

Alia focused on the fight in front of her. She shook her head. "No, Princess."

Delia sighed. "What if you pretend you are the king? What then?"

Alia blinked at her. "Let me try." She took a breath and assumed a crouched fighting stance.

Delia watched as Alia did what she'd been doing. The shield maiden shifted minutely, hands and arms twitching.

After a moment she stood up. "No Princess. It doesn't seem to work that way."

"Thank you for trying."

Delia took a breath and blew it out. Her hopes to use Alia's magic sight for strikes were dashed. Besides, even if she could see a blow not meant for her, they'd never talked about whether Alia could send her thoughts to her. She didn't even know if she could send thoughts herself. Her fingers drummed against the sword's pommel. Both Ucheni and Iyuno were using swords. Magical, Delia supposed. Iyuno was driving her father back. It was if her uncle were getting stronger. She looked again at his soldiers. There was no smoke from a fire. Where was he getting his strength?

Suddenly, her father's foot caught on something as he was stepping back and he went to one knee. Iyuno raised his sword and before Delia could scream, he brought the sword down. Her father paused, sword half-raised. The army went silent. A gash appeared at the base of his neck. His sword dropped, in seeming slow motion, as her father followed.

Then, she did scream. "FAAATHERRRRR!"

She ran out onto the field, fireballs in both hands. She had flung them at Iyuno before her father had finished falling.

Iyuno swung his sword around and slid it into its scabbard as he held up a hand. Delia was knocked back, falling into the long grass. She turned on her magical sight. Now was not the time to be emotional, she thought as she rolled to her feet. She used her invisible heat force but the force bounced from Iyuno's magical shield.

Delia made a shield for herself and glanced back at her army's line. *Her* army, came the flash of thought. Alia had lit the fire. Delia pulled its strength to her, then faced Iyuno.

"So, pup. You think you're ready to face me?"

"Face you I will, evil one." She moved into a fighting stance. "You've killed my father."

"Not much of a father, handing you over to slavers," he said as he circled.

She watched as he moved. Where was he getting his power? She flung the sleeping spell at him. It splashed against his shield.

He threw another fireball while swinging his sword at her. She stepped outside the swing as his fireball hit her shield.

This could go on forever, she thought. *Each of us is getting power from fire. How long can I pull on that and survive?* His constant barrage of fireballs, force balls and other tricks she'd never seen were keeping her busy but she did her best, now that she was closer, to see where his power was coming from, while still putting up some resistance.

A flash at his feet drew her attention. What sort of magic was that? She looked closer as she chanted the sleeping spell and threw a fireball. *The ground?* He was getting power from the earth? How could that be?

Where was Sisruo? Shouldn't Iyuno's hundred elves be asleep by now?

She scrambled as Iyuno pressed his attack. He was powerful, and her magical shield was taking a beating. Delia drew more heavily from the fire. He had to know what she was doing. Why didn't he try to stop her?

She tried everything she knew, including throwing up a protection spell around him, but she didn't have the skills and training he had. He was going to kill her, too, if she didn't do something.

He taunted her again. "You've developed some small skill, niece. Congratulations." He delivered an invisible blow as he used his other hand to try and force her off of her feet.

Delia didn't answer. At his feet were flashes of light. What was he drawing from? "Die, traitor."

He laughed and somehow, clapped his hands together, creating a gong sound. Then he took a step back. Now what?

Screams from her army sounded behind her, as in front of her, behind Iyuno, the ground opened up and orcs came streaming from the holes. She stared. Orcs? Weren't they all dead?

"You've broken the protocol, Uncle."

He laughed. "Winning is winning, niece."

She struck out, anger washing through her as orcs came racing across the field. Delia doubled her efforts as she used the anger to fuel her magic. She wasn't sure just what she was doing, but fire and lightning burst from her finger tips. Delia swatted at her uncle. A force ball like none other she'd ever done flew from her left hand, making him stagger. She pulled power from the fire. Ah, his fire was underground. That was it. Delia pulled power from that as well.

She charged as the first of the orcs reached her. They swirled around her as though she were not there. That wasn't what she'd expected. Her army, though, were in the fight of their lives. Iyuno was not so lucky. Her charge took her right up to him. She held him, magically, with one hand as she drew her sword. "You killed my father!" She ran him through, twice, three times. Once more, as he lay on the ground. She pulled her sword from his body and began chanting the sleeping spell and swinging at orcs.

She was half way back to her own lines when she realized Alia was beside her, taking out orc after orc. The field was littered with bodies, orcs mostly, but elves as well. Delia's anger exploded and she seemed to swell, larger and larger, as she charged after the orcs. When she'd finally killed the last one she found, Alia was calling to her.

"Princess! Princess! Stop! It's over."

Delia drew a breath and blinked. "Over?" She felt shrunken and old.

"Over, Princess. You've won."

Delia removed her helmet and pushed loose, sweat-soaked hair back from her face and looked around. "Over." She sank to the ground, exhausted.

CHAPTER 43

Alia called for help, and two elves she didn't know took Delia back to the king's tent. "No." She pushed away from the tent. "My tent."

"But Your Majesty," Alia began.

"No!" Delia shook her head. "My tent."

Alia directed them to Delia's tent. "Get the mage," Alia directed one of them. To the other she said, "Get hot water and cloths."

Alia got Delia's breastplate off and her boots. By then, water arrived in a basin with cloths. She washed Delia and put her clean shirt and trousers on her, then let her lie down and sleep.

When Delia woke, the table had a single candle and Alia was dozing, head propped on her fist at the table. She sat up. The small noise woke Alia.

"Majesty." She leapt from the chair. "What do you need?

"I need to know what's happening."

Alia ducked her head. Everyone is at Master Kaepli's tent."

Delia put on socks and boots, having to shoo Alia away.

"I've been dressing my own feet for years, Alia. Leave me be."

Alia complied but fidgeted in the corner of the tent while she waited.

"Is there anything to eat?" Delia asked.

"I'll bring it to the mage's tent."

"Good."

Alia insisted on walking her there before going to get the food. When she entered, everyone, including Master Kaepli, stood. Delia sighed to herself. *So this is what is was going to be like from now on?* "Reports?"

"We're glad to see you recovered, Prin, excuse me, Majesty." Kaepli bowed.

"Thank you. How are our forces from the passes?"

He motioned for her to come to the map table. Juner stepped aside. Kaya nodded her greeting and Delia gave her a smile. Mysteso and Neoni weren't in the tent but Lord Enaur was. "Tell me."

Kaepli took a deep breath. "Orcs, Majesty. We had no idea any were left."

"There are fewer now," Delia said. The very thought of the ugly creatures she'd had to fight made her skin crawl. "My uncle apparently made a pact with them." She shook her head. "I'll never understand it."

"Agreed."

"And Captain Catari? Neoni? Mysteso?"

"Catari took heavy losses at the south pass, Majesty. He was severely injured and lost all but one of his men and many of ours."

A quick thought of sorrow flashed through her mind. She swallowed what seemed like a huge lump in her throat. She took a breath and decided she'd grieve later. "And the north pass?"

"Neoni, too, received a wound, but not too bad." He sighed. "Mysteso was killed. They had orcs there as well."

She hadn't known either of them long, but still, a pang of grief, sharp as a blade, went through her heart. Delia swallowed back tears. She was a queen now; tears were for private times. Still, it took a moment for her to find her voice. "My uncle's forces were stopped, though?"

"Yes, Majesty."

"And Sisruo?"

"He took the brunt of the orc attack at the field, Majesty."

Delia stared at him. "And?"

"He, Couran, and Palen were all injured. They're in the sick tent."

Alive, she thought. *Still alive.* "I'll have to go visit them."

"Yes, Majesty."

Alia came in with a plate of roast meat and vegetables. "Majesty. Your dinner."

The aroma made Delia's stomach growl. Apparently, power from fire didn't satisfy that need. She sat down, the plate on top of the maps, and ate as though she'd not eaten in days. "Go on."

"We've lost nearly a thousand elves, Majesty."

"And where are Nethene and Ceinno?"

"Dead, Majesty."

Delia nodded. Painfully, she hoped, but kept that to herself. "Has word been sent to my mother?"

"Not yet, Majesty." Kaepli licked his lips. "We await your order."

Of course, she thought as she ate the last bite of the roast. "Send word that Father has died but that I have survived."

"Where is Father's body?" She stood up.

"In his tent, Majesty."

"I'll go see him."

Kaepli bowed.

Delia left the tent, Alia behind her. After her, trailed two elven guards. *I'll have to get used to that, too, I suppose.*

Two guards outside of the king's tent door, one on each side. They saluted as she passed and she saluted back. Alia stayed outside.

Inside she found her father, washed and dressed in the best robes he had with him, lying in state on a makeshift table, draped in long, cotton cloth. His cloak was wrapped around him and four large candles stood at the corners of the makeshift byre. Gold coins weighted his eyes and a crown of flowers was on his head.

Delia rested her fingertips on the cloth, not touching the body. *It's too soon. I didn't get to know you. Why? Why?* Tears fell as the pain in her chest grew. *So much time, wasted. Damn Iyuno. Damn Nethene and Ceinno. Why?* The tears fell and fell, but quietly, so the elves outside couldn't hear. She didn't know how long she'd stood there, but finally the tears stopped and she wiped her eyes with her sleeve. Delia sniffed and left.

"Sick tent," she said when she got outside. Alia raced ahead as her two guards followed.

Once there she made the round of cots, greeting each elf in turn. Finally, she reached Sisruo, Couran, and Relan. "I see you survived."

"And you, Princess." Couran said.

Pelan reached over and smacked his brother. "Majesty, you dolt." He looked at Delia. "Excuse my brother, Majesty. He's had the sense knocked out of him."

"I understand. I had the sense knocked out of me today, too. "I'm glad you three are all right," she said, looking at Sisruo. "May you all heal quickly."

She spoke to Kaya. "I'm glad you are here to help them."

"Rest, Majesty. You've had a bit of a day as well."

All of a sudden, Delia felt like an old, used-up rag. "Perhaps you're right." She took Kaya's hand and kissed her on the cheek. "Thank you."

"You're welcome."

Delia went back to her tent. "Alia. I need to sleep. Unless we're under attack, let me rest."

"Yes, Majesty." She bowed and backed out of the tent.

Delia sat down and pulled off her boots. That didn't mean she was alone. There'd be someone outside the tent all the time, listening for her least command. She pulled the blanket over herself and turned on her side, asleep in a moment.

CHAPTER 44

When they arrived at the palace, Mage Kaepli took down the protective spell and they all entered.

Delia went to her rooms over the objection of Master Kaepli. "But Your Majesty, you belong in the king's rooms."

"Not until I talk to my mother. That will be the end of it." She went in and closed the door. Outside she could hear two guards take their positions on either side, and sighed. They were just as tired as she was but there they were, standing guard. All she wanted was a proper bath and a huge dinner. But the few cooks the army had with them wouldn't have had time to heat water, let alone cook anything. She remembered the state of the kitchen. Totally cleaned out. Someone would have to go hunting or something before anyone had anything other than camp rations to eat. She hoped her mother had supplies.

It was a week before her mother arrived.

Delia was in the courtyard to meet her. She gave her mother a hug and a kiss on the cheek after she'd dismounted. "Mother. I'm so sorry." Her mother looked pale and thin in her white mourning dress.

Ralae patted Delia on the cheek. "I'm so proud of you. You defeated our enemy. There is much to be happy for."

Delia walked with her to Ralae's rooms. "Rest, mother. May I get you anything?"

"Later, daughter. We'll go see your father before the burial."

Delia nodded. "Let me know when you're ready. I'll escort you."

Ralae nodded. "Thank you."

That evening they went to the throneroom together. Held under a spell, Ucheni was in his finest robes, his crown upon his head. Candles surrounded the body and an honor guard of twelve surrounded him. Ralae put her hand on his. "He loved you. Very much."

"I know. He showed it in every way."

Ralae sniffed and used a delicate handkerchief to wipe her eyes. "He died too young."

"Iyuno paid for that."

Ralae turned to Delia. "I heard stories."

Delia shrugged. "He treated with orcs, Mother."

Ralae sighed. "True."

They had a quiet supper in the Queen Mother's rooms and Delia took her leave early.

Three months later, the coronation was held. Ralae was still in her rooms, but Delia had moved into her father's apartment. It seemed weird to her. She stood in front of a floor-length mirror as Alia stood by and servants fussed with the coronation gown. It had been less than a year since Corpet, the caravan master, had given her that elegant blue gown to wear. Slave to queen in that short amount of time. It didn't seem real.

Alia nodded. "You look beautiful."

Delia studied her reflection. Her hair was still very short

but the servants had found a scarf that provided enough bulk that the crown could go on her head. She teleported a mug of tea to her hand from a nearby table. It was a trick she'd developed one day by accident when a quill was just out of reach. Alia's eyebrow rose. "Just in private, Ali. It seems silly to have you fetch it when I can just call it."

Alia shook her head. "As you will, Majesty."

Delia rolled her eyes. Alia was a stickler. Fortunately, Kaya still had a sense of humor, as did Couran, Pelan and Sisruo. She needed friends and confidantes, not masters. "I'll not do it in public. I promise."

The ceremony lasted too long, Delia thought, but her mother looked pleased and that's all she could hope for.

She thought about Captain Catari. He had died in the sick tent, some poison he'd gotten from orc darts. Her thoughts turned to her mother. One day, she would move out of the next-door apartments, replaced by a husband. That might be Sisruo. He'd passed his exams after he'd healed and was now a Master Mage himself. They would be a powerful couple, if it all worked out. She was still too young to marry, though. Another hundred years or so to get to know him, and her people, and her culture. It would pass in no time.

Thank you for reading.

THANK YOU FOR READING

Thank you for taking the time to read Slave Elf. If you enjoyed it, please consider telling your friends and family and posting a short review. Word of mouth is an author's best friend and much appreciated.

I offer a free story to anyone signing up for my newsletter, Connie's Random Thoughts which can be found at https://www.conniesrandomthoughts.com/newsletter.

ABOUT THE AUTHOR

Connie Cockrell grew up in upstate New York, just outside of Gloversville. She now lives in Payson, Arizona with her husband: biking, gardening, and playing bunko. Cockrell began writing in response to a challenge from her daughter in October 2011 and has been hooked ever since. She writes about whatever comes into her head so her books could be in any genre. She's published nineteen books so far and has been included in six different anthologies, and has been published on EveryDayStories.com and FrontierTales.com. Connie's always on the lookout for a good story idea. Beware! You may be the next one!

Did you enjoy Slave Elf? Sign up to be notified of Cockrell's next book at her newsletter: https://conniesrandomthoughts.com/newsletter.

EXCERPT OF MYSTERY AT THE REUNION

Chapter 1

Jean exited the elevator and headed to the Starlight lounge at the Silver Miner hotel and casino where she'd arrived to attend the first reunion of the Combined Joint Force Command squadron AG2017. She'd been looking forward to this for months. Much as she loved Karen, her best friend in Greyson, Arizona, she missed the friends she'd made in Afghanistan. There was something about those ties to people she'd served with under difficult circumstances.

When she arrived, the lounge was busy, tables were full, and people were standing in small groups all around the room. Not closed to the public, she showed her badge to the bartender. "Pinot Grigio, please." He nodded and moved off to pour her drink. The first hour was open bar, part of the reunion cost she'd paid. After that, it was pay your own way. She looked around. Jean recognized several people and was looking forward to catching up. From the Facebook group she and they belonged to, she knew several, like her, who had reached their retirement age and had moved on to other jobs.

Some jobs related to the work they did in the Air Force, Navy, Marines, or Army, some not.

The bartender delivered her drink and Jean gave him a smile and a dollar tip. She joined the group standing on the far side of the room. "Hey, people!"

"Jean!" Justin Romero clapped her on the shoulder. "Great to see you."

"You still in supply?" Jean asked.

"Yeah, but with Hellerman, you remember. They had all the building contracts back in the box."

"I remember." Her mind went back to the investigation she'd endured just a few months earlier. She made a mental note to talk to him about it later. Jean traded hellos with the others in the group; Stephanie French, Norman Heller, and Brandon Rivers. "It has been forever. I haven't seen you post on the page, Norm. What are you up to lately?"

"Ugh. I don't have time to hardly brush my teeth let alone keep up with social media. Took a job with the Department of Defense doing quality control on foreign contractors." He rolled his eyes and shook his head. "It seemed so simple in the interview. Lots of travel to exotic places. Blech. I'm exhausted from jet lag most of the time."

"That sucks, old buddy." Brandon gave Norm's arm a light punch. "I'm still in though I've only got a year left. I'm cooling my heels in Anchorage, Joint Force Base Elmendorf-Richardson. Nothing exceptional in my project management projects. I'm already contacting some of the multi-nationals, looking for a high-paying gig."

Jean never thought much of Brandon. One of the only other project managers in her unit in Afghanistan, his projects were always behind schedule or over budget or both. "What about you, Steph?" she asked. "Plans for when you get out?"

"Not yet." Stephanie sipped her wine—a red of some

kind. "Doing admin is great in the military, but it's kind of hard to make that carry over into civilian life. Being an executive secretary could potentially be high-paying, but I'm not sure I want to go in that direction."

Jean patted her on the shoulder. "I'm sure you'll think of something. I remember the time it was just you and me in the office. The commander was stuck out back of beyond and the First Sergeant was out and so was everyone else. It was just you and me and the phones started ringing off the hook because of an imminent attack. And you were just a couple of months into your tour. Dang, you were cool under pressure."

Stephanie grinned. "Thanks. Inside I was screaming, 'Oh God! Oh God! Oh God!'"

"It never showed. You'll be great at whatever you want to do."

Stephanie lifted her glass in salute. "Here's to all of us. Home in one piece."

"Here, here," they all repeated and drank.

The group broke up and each person drifted to other tables and standing groups. Jean joined the nearest, where Kiko Johnson, Ian Waring, and Soren Stewart were standing. "Hi, everyone."

Kiko slid an arm around Jean's waist. "I have missed you. I've got two years left in and you've been out forever!"

"Yeah. Just after my last tour. How are you?"

"I'm good. My last assignments haven't been as good as that last one with you. It was just a great group!"

"It was." Jean looked at the other two. "How are you, Ian? I know you got out just after I did."

He nodded, squat glass of what Jean suspected was bourbon, his drink of choice back in the day, in his hand. "I got out of networking. Went back to school and got my nursing degree. I'm still on duty around the clock but I'm helping people. I like it."

"Good for you! I never knew you weren't interested in keeping the network up. IT pays pretty good."

"It can." He gave a small shrug. "But I was tired of working in a refrigerated room all alone. This is better." He turned to Soren. "What about you?"

Soren laughed. "I'm a travel blogger. You believe that? I travel, write about it, earn money. Best job ever!"

The whole group laughed. Jean asked, "How do you make money at that?"

"Monetize your blog and vlog. It's a whole thing. I have thousands of followers."

"You are going to haftta tell us how that works," Kiko said. "I could get into that."

Another person joined the group. "Hey!"

Jean turned. The smile on her face evaporated. "Dwight." Her tone of voice made the Jovian ice planets seem warm.

He greeted everyone else. Kiko was the first to make her excuses. The others followed rapidly after her, leaving Jean alone with Dwight.

Dwight snorted. "Way to clear a room, Jean."

Jean glared, swallowed what was left of her wine and went back to the bar. "Pinot Grigio, please."

Behind her Dwight said, "Crown Royal."

She ground her teeth together. He still couldn't catch a hint. Her walking away should have been enough.

"So. What are you up to now-a-days? Still in Arizona?" He put an elbow on the bar and leaned into it, one foot on the rail, watching her.

Jean sighed. "Yes. I'm still in Arizona. You still in Massachusetts?"

"Yep. A new company, though. The city of Boston, actually."

Jean's eyes narrowed. "Seems like a pay cut."

He shrugged and as the bartender approached, pulled a wad of cash from his pocket and peeled off a five for the man, dropping it on the bar. He took a long swallow of his drink.

"What's going on, Dwight. You're still transparent."

He swallowed the last of his drink while signalling the bartender for another. "You know. Another day, another project."

Jean tilted her head as she studied him. "Something else." Her eyes went wide. "The Twinkie divorced you!"

Dwight shook his head and sighed. "I wish you wouldn't call her 'the twinkie.'" He ran his hand through his hair. He always did that when he was frustrated. The same move their son made.

"What happened?" Jean was surprised she wasn't more gleeful. Well, maybe a little. She sipped her wine and waited.

"I don't know. We were working our asses off, hardly time to see each other even on the weekends. You know what it's like on a big project. Anyway, a year and a half ago she says she's had enough. It's no fun anymore."

Jean repressed a snort. That was just about what he had told her when he left her standing, slack-jawed, in their foyer back in Connecticut.

"She said I was boring and we never went out anymore." He sighed again. "I did my best. I was pulling in great money, but she took off with a guy just five years older than her." He took a deep breath. "Anyway. My drinking went up, my performance dropped off, the company let me go when the project went over budget."

"So that's why you're working for the city?"

Dwight nodded. "I have all I can do to pay both alimonies."

The bartender brought his drink and Dwight sipped it this time.

Jean sipped her wine. "No. I'm not going to relieve you of my alimony. You left me, remember? Just left me standing the hall while you loaded your suitcase into her little red sports car and drove off. Took all of the money out of our bank accounts, too, as I remember."

That brought back the still raw feelings of the day. She sniffed back imminent tears and took a huge swallow of wine. Then she used the little cocktail napkin to blow her nose. "You were a bastard and I've had all I could do not to bad mouth you to our son."

Dwight took another deep breath. "I know. I appreciate that. Though, since Jim's had his own family, we don't talk so much."

Jean sniffed again. "I don't feel sorry for you at all. You deserve all the karma you're getting back."

Dwight had both hands on the bar. He tapped one against it. "You're right, I suppose. Yeah. Right." He picked up his drink and walked away.

Mystery at the Reunion will be out in 2019.